Dear Reader,

As I write my books, I work with what Edith Wharton described as "a heartbeat at my feet." Mitzi is totally devoted. She's often smelly, she's sometimes scratchy and she's occasionally impatient. She doesn't understand that I need to finish the next scene—she wants walks. If you ask if I could write without a dog at my feet, I'll confess I've never tried. Before Mitzi, there was Harry. Before Harry, Chloe, Pete, Radar, Buster…

So finally, after years of writing *with* dogs, I've decided to write *about* dogs. Dogs I've known. Dogs I've loved. Only the names have been changed, to protect the not so innocent.

Kleppy is a kleptomaniac, a fabulous thieving dog. Living with him is a roller coaster of a ride, always keeping just one tail length from the law. But he charms my lovely heroine, lawyer Abigail Callahan, into rescuing him, and shows her how to follow her heart right into the arms of the man she hasn't dared to love—gorgeous cop Raff Finn.

Welcome to Banksia Bay, where lost dogs heal lonely hearts! Kleppy is the first of many. Enjoy.

Marion Lennox

BANKSIA BAY

Where lost dogs heal lonely hearts…

Marion Lennox brings you two wonderfully warm, witty, emotional and uplifting stories with happy endings you'll never forget.

Step into Banskia Bay, a picturesque seaside town where hearts are made whole and dreams really can come true! With the help of a few mischievous little dogs, two couples get together and find that they are in for journeys they had never expected….

Abby and the Bachelor Cop

Lawyer and bride-to-be Abigail Callahan has her life mapped out. Then gorgeous bad-boy-turned-cop Raff Finn reenters Abby's life, landing her with an adorable homeless dog called Kleppy and a whole lot of trouble….

Misty and the Single Dad

Teacher Misty has aspirations to leave Banksia Bay, but then Nicholas Holt, tall, dark and deliciously bronzed, turns up in her classroom with his adorable little son, Bailey, and an injured stray spaniel in tow. Soon Misty has to make a choice: follow her dreams…or her heart?

MARION LENNOX

Abby and the Bachelor Cop

BANKSIA BAY

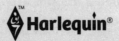

TORONTO NEW YORK LONDON
AMSTERDAM PARIS SYDNEY HAMBURG
STOCKHOLM ATHENS TOKYO MILAN MADRID
PRAGUE WARSAW BUDAPEST AUCKLAND

Recycling programs
for this product may
not exist in your area.

ISBN-13: 978-0-373-17731-8

ABBY AND THE BACHELOR COP

First North American Publication 2011

Copyright © 2011 by Marion Lennox

This edition published by arrangement with Harlequin Books S.A.

For questions and comments about the quality of this book please contact us at Customer_eCare@Harlequin.ca.

www.eHarlequin.com

Printed in U.S.A.

Marion Lennox is a country girl, born on an Australian dairy farm. She moved on—mostly because the cows just weren't interested in her stories! Married to a "very special doctor," Marion writes for the Medical Romance and Harlequin Romance lines. (She used a different name for each category for a while—readers looking for her past Mills & Boon Harlequin Romance novels should search for author Trisha David, as well.) She's now had more than seventy-five romance novels accepted for publication.

In her non-writing life Marion cares for kids, cats, dogs, chickens and goldfish. She travels, she fights her rampant garden (she's losing) and her house dust (she's lost).

Having spun in circles for the first part of her life, she's now stepped back from her "other" career, which was teaching statistics at her local university. Finally she's reprioritized her life, figured what's important and discovered the joys of deep baths, romance and chocolate.

Preferably all at the same time!

With huge thanks to
the wonderful Kelly Hunter, who gave me Kleppy,
to the fabulous Anne Gracie, and to
all the Maytoners, whose friendships
bring my stories to life.

To Radar, who was Trouble. I look back on
every moment with laughter and with love

CHAPTER ONE

IF YOU couldn't be useful at the scene of an accident, you should leave. Onlookers only caused trouble.

Banksia Bay's Animal Welfare van had been hit from behind. Dogs were everywhere. People were yelling at each other. Esther Ford was having hysterics.

Abigail Callahan, however, had been travelling at a safe enough distance to avoid the crash. She'd managed to stop before her little red sports car hit anything, and she'd done all she could.

She'd checked no one was hurt. She'd hugged Esther, she'd tried to calm her down and she'd phoned Esther's son who, she hoped, might be better at coping with hysterics than she was. She'd carried someone's crumpled fender to the side of the road. She'd even tried to catch a dog. Luckily, she'd failed. She wasn't good with dogs.

Now, blessedly, Emergency Services had arrived. Banksia Bay Emergency Services took the shape of Rafferty Finn, local cop, so it was definitely time for Abby to leave.

Stay away from Raff Finn.

It wasn't past history making her go. She was doing the right thing.

She tried to back her car so she could turn, but the crowd of onlookers was blocking her way. She touched her horn and Raff glared at her.

How else could she make people move? She did not need to be here. She looked down at her briefcase and thought about the notes inside that she knew had to be in court—now. Then she glanced back at Raff and she thought… She thought…

She thought Rafferty Finn looked toe-curlingly sexy.

Which was ridiculous.

Abby had fallen for Raff when she was eight. It was more than time she was over it. She *was* over it. She was so over it she was engaged to be married. To Philip.

When Raff had been ten years old, which was when Abby had developed her first crush on him, he'd been skinny, freckled and his red hair had spiked straight up. Twenty years on, skinny had given way to tall, tanned and ripped. His thick curls had darkened to burned copper, and his freckles had merged to an all-over tan. His gorgeous green eyes, with dangerous mischief lurking within, had the capacity to make her catch her breath.

But right now it was his uniform that was causing problems. His uniform was enough to make a girl go right back to feeling as she had at eight years old.

Raff was directing drivers. He was calm, authoritative and far more sexy than any man had a right to be.

'Henrietta, hold that Dalmatian before it knocks Mrs Ford over. Roger, quit yelling at Mrs Ford. You drove into the dog van, not Mrs Ford, and it doesn't make a bit of difference that she was going too slow. Back your Volvo up and get it off the road.'

Do not look at Raff Finn, she told herself. Do not.

The man is trouble.

She turned and tried again to reverse her car. Why wouldn't people move?

Someone was thumping on her window. The door of her car swung open. She swivelled and her heart did a back flip. Raff was standing over her—six foot two of lethal cop. With dog.

'I need your help, Abby,' he growled and, before she could react, there was a dog in her car. On her knees.

'I need you to take him to the vet,' Raff said. 'Now.'

The vet?

The local veterinary clinic was half a mile away, on the outskirts of town.

But she wasn't given a chance to argue. Raff slammed her car door closed and started helping Mrs Ford steer to the kerb.

There was a dog on her knee.

Abby's grandmother had once owned a shortbread tin adorned with a picture of a dog called Greyfriars Bobby. According to legend—or Gran—Bobby was famous for guarding his master's grave for almost fourteen years through the bleakest of Edinburgh's winters. This dog looked his twin. He was smallish but not a toy. His coat was wiry and a bit scruffy, sort of sand-coloured. One of his ears was a bit floppy.

His eyebrows were too long.

Did dogs have eyebrows?

He looked up at her as if he was just as stunned as she was.

What was wrong with him? Why did he need to go to the vet?

He wasn't bleeding.

She was due in court in ten minutes. Help.

What to do with a dog?

She put a hand on his head and gave him a tentative pat. Very tentative. If she moved him, maybe she'd hurt him. Maybe he'd hurt her.

He wiggled his head to the side and she tried scratching behind his ear. That seemed to be appreciated. His eyes were huge, brown and limpid. He had a raggedy tail and he gave it a tentative wag.

His eyes didn't leave hers. His eyes were…were…

Let's cut out the emotion here, she told herself hastily. This dog is nothing to do with you.

She fumbled under the dog for the door catch and climbed out of the car. The dog's backside sort of slumped as she lifted him. Actually, both ends slumped.

She carried him back to Raff. The little dog looked up at her and his tail still wagged. It seemed a half-hearted wag, as if he wasn't at all sure where he was but he sort of hoped things might be okay.

She felt exactly the same.

Raff was back in the middle of the crashed cars. 'Raff, I can't...' she called.

Raff had given up trying to get Mrs Ford to steer. He had hold of her steering wheel and was steering himself, pushing at the same time, moving the car to the kerb all by himself. 'Can't what?' he demanded.

'I can't take this dog anywhere.'

'Henrietta says it's okay,' Raff snapped. 'It's the only one she's caught. She's trying to round up the others. Come on, Abby, the road's clear—how hard is this? Just take him to the vet.'

'I'm due in court in ten minutes.'

'So am I.' Raff shoved Mrs Ford's car another few feet and then paused for breath. 'If you think I've spent years getting Wallace Baxter behind bars, just to see you and your prissy boyfriend get him off because I can't make it...'

'Cut it out, Raff.'

'Cut what out?'

'He's not prissy,' she snapped. 'And he's not my boyfriend. You know he's my fiancé.'

'Your fiancé. I stand corrected. But he's definitely prissy. I'll bet he's sitting in court right now, in his smart suit and silk tie—not like me, out here getting my hands dirty. Case for the prosecution—me and the time I can spare after work. Case for the defence—you and Philip and weeks of paid preparation. Two lawyers against one cop.'

'There's the Crown Prosecutor...'

'Who's eighty. Who sleeps instead of listening. This'll be a no-brainer, even if you don't show.' He shoved the car a bit further. 'But I'll be there, whether you like it or not. Meanwhile, take the dog to the vet's.'

'You're saying you want me to take the dog to the vet's—to keep me out of court?'

'I'm saying take the dog to the vet's because there's no one else,' he snapped. 'Your car's the only one still roadworthy. I'll radio Justice Weatherby to ask for a half hour delay. That'll get us both there on time. Get to the vet's and get back.'

'But I don't do dogs,' she wailed. 'Raff…'

'You don't want to get your suit dirty?'

'That's not fair. This isn't about my suit.' Or not very. 'It's just… What's wrong with him? I mean… I can't look after him. What if he bites?'

Raff sighed. 'He won't bite,' he said, speaking to her as if she were eight years old again. 'He's a pussycat. His name's Kleppy. He's Isaac Abrahams' Cairn Terrier and he's on his way to be put down. Put him on your passenger seat and Fred'll take him out at the other end. All I'm asking you to do is deliver him.'

It was twelve minutes to ten on a beautiful morning in Banksia Bay. The sun was warm on her face. The sea was glittering beyond the harbour and the mountain behind the town was blue with the haze of a still autumn morning. The sounds of the traffic chaos were lessening as Raff's attempts at restoring order took effect.

Abby stood motionless, her arms full of dog, and Raff's words replayed in her head.

He's Isaac Abrahams' Cairn Terrier and he's on his way to be put down.

She knew Isaac or, rather, she'd known him. The old man had lived a mile or so out of town, up on Black Mountain where…well, where she didn't go any more. Isaac had died six weeks ago and she was handling probate. Isaac's daughter in Sydney had been into the office a couple of times, busy and efficient in her disposing of Isaac's belongings.

There'd been no talk of a dog.

'Can you get your car off the road?' Raff said. 'You're blocking traffic.'

She was blocking traffic? But she gazed around and realised she was.

Somehow, magically, Raff had every other car to the side

of the road. Raff was like that. He ordered and people obeyed. There were a couple of tow trucks arriving but already cars could get through.

There was no problem. All she had to do was get in the car—with dog—and drive to the vet's.

But…to take a dog to be put down?

'Henrietta should do this,' she said, looking round for the lady she knew ran the Animal Shelter. But Raff put his hands on his cop hips and she thought any minute now he'd get ugly.

'Henrietta has a van full of dogs to find,' he snapped.

'But she runs the Animal Shelter.'

'So?'

'So that's where he needs to go. Surely not to be put down.'

Raff's face hardened. She knew that look. Life hadn't been easy for Raff—she knew that, too. When he was up against it…well, he did what he had to do.

'Abby, I know this dog—I've known him for years,' he told her, and his voice was suddenly bleak. 'I took him to the Animal Shelter the night Isaac died. His daughter doesn't want him and neither does anyone else. The only guy who loves him is Isaac's gardener, and Lionel lives in a rooming house. There's no way he can keep him. The Shelter's full to bursting. Kleppy's had six weeks and the Shelter can't keep him any longer. Fred's waiting. The injection will be quick. Don't drag it out, Abby. Deliver the dog, and I'll see you in court.'

'But…'

'Just do it.' And he turned his back on her and started directing tow trucks.

He'd just given Abigail Callahan a dog and she looked totally flummoxed.

She looked adorable.

Yeah, well, it was high time he stopped thinking Abby was adorable. As a teenager, Abby had seemed a piece of him—a part of his whole—but she'd watched him with condemnation for ten years now. She'd changed from the laughing kid she used to be—from his adoring shadow—to someone he no longer liked very much.

He'd killed her brother.

Raff had finally come to terms with that long-ago tragedy—or he'd accepted it as much as he ever could—but he'd killed a part of her. How did a man get past that?

It was time he accepted that he never could.

What sort of name was Kleppy for a dog?

He shouldn't have told her its name.

Only she would have figured it. The dog had a blue plastic collar, obviously standard Animal Welfare issue, but whoever had attached it had reattached his tag, as if they were leaving him a bit of personality to the end.

Kleppy.

The name had been scratched by hand on the back of what looked like a medal. Abby set the dog on her passenger seat—he wagged his tail again and turned round twice and settled—and she couldn't help turning over his tag.

It was a medal. She recognised it and stared.

Old Man Abrahams had done something pretty impressive in the war. She'd heard rumours but she'd never had confirmation.

This was more than confirmation. A medal of honour, an amazing medal of honour—hanging on the collar of a scruffy, homeless mutt called Kleppy.

Uh-oh. He was looking up at her again now. His brown eyes were huge.

Six weeks in the Animal Shelter. She'd gone there once on some sort of school excursion. Concrete cells with a tiny exercise yard. Too many dogs, gazing up at her with hope she couldn't possibly match.

'The people who run this do a wonderful job,' she remembered her teacher saying. 'But they can't save every dog. If you ask your parents for a pet for Christmas you need to understand a dog can live for twenty years. Every dog deserves a loving home, boys and girls.'

She'd been what? Thirteen? She remembered looking at the dogs and starting to cry.

And she also remembered Raff—of course it was Raff— patting her awkwardly on the shoulder. 'Hey, it's okay, Abby. There'll be a fairy godmother somewhere. I reckon all these dogs'll be claimed by tea time.'

'Yeah, probably by your grandmother,' someone had said, not unkindly. 'How many dogs do you have, Finn?'

'Seven,' he'd said and the Welfare lady had pursed her lips.

'See, that's the problem,' she said. 'No family should have more than two.'

'So you ought to bring five in,' someone else told Raff and Raff had gone quiet.

You ought to bring five in. To be put down? Maybe that was what Philip would think, Abby decided, though she couldn't remember Philip being there. But even then Philip had been a stickler for rules.

As were her parents.

'We don't want an abandoned dog,' they'd said in horror that night all those years ago. 'Why would you want someone else's cast-off?'

She needed to remember her parents' advice right now, for Isaac Abrahams' cast-off was in her car. Wearing a medal of valour.

'Move the car, Abby.' Raff's voice was inexorable. She glanced up and he was filling her windscreen.

'I don't want…'

'You don't always get what you want,' he growled. 'I thought you were old enough to figure that out. While you're figuring, shift the car.'

'But…'

'Or I'll get you towed for obstructing traffic,' he snapped. 'No choice, lady. Move.'

* * *

So all she had to do was take one dog to the vet's and get herself to court. How hard was that?

She drove and Kleppy stayed motionless on the passenger seat and looked at her. Looking as if he trusted her with his life.

She felt sick.

This wasn't her responsibility. Kleppy belonged to an old guy who'd died six weeks ago. His daughter didn't want him. No one else had claimed him, so the sensible, humane thing to do was have him put down.

But what if…? What if…?

Oh, help, what she thinking?

She was getting married on Saturday week. To Philip.

Nine days.

Her tiny house was full of wedding presents. Her wedding gown was hanging in the hall, a vision of beaded ivory satin. She'd made it herself, every stitch. She loved that dress.

This dog would walk past it and she'd have dog hair on ivory silk…

Well, that was a dumb thing to think. For this dog to walk past it, he'd have to be in her house, and this dog was headed to the vet's. To be put down.

He looked up at her and whimpered. His paw came out and touched her knee.

Her heart turned over. Nooooo.

It took five minutes to drive to the vet's. Kleppy's paw rested against her knee the whole time.

She pulled up. Kleppy wasn't shaking. She was.

Fred came out to meet her. The elderly vet looked grim. He went straight to the passenger door. Tugged it open.

'Raff rang to say you were coming,' he said, lifting Kleppy out. 'Thanks for bringing him. Do you know when the rest are coming?'

'I… Henrietta was trying to catch them. How many?'

'More than I want to think about,' Fred said grimly. 'Three months from Christmas, puppies stop being cute. Not your call, though. I'll deal with him from here.'

Kleppy lay limp in Fred's arms. He looked back at her.

The paw on her knee…

Help. Help, help, help.

'It'll be quick?'

Fred glanced at her, brows snapping. Abby had gone to school with Fred's daughter. He knew her well. 'Don't,' he said.

'Don't what?'

'Think about it. Get on with your life. Nine days till the wedding?'

'I…yes.'

'Then you've enough on your plate without worrying about stray dogs. Not that you and Philip would ever want a dog. You're not dog people.'

'What…what do you mean?'

'Dogs are mess,' he said. 'Not your style. You guys might qualify for a goldfish. See you later, love. Happy wedding if I don't see you before.'

He turned away. She could no longer see Kleppy.

She could feel him.

His eyes…

Help. Help, help, help.

She was a goldfish person? She'd never even had a goldfish.

A paw on her knee…

He reached the door before she broke.

'Fred?'

The vet turned. Kleppy was still slumped.

'Yes?'

'I can't bear this,' she said. 'Can you…can you take him in, check him out for damage and then give him back to me?'

'Give him back?'

'Yes.'

'You want him?'

'He's my wedding present to me.' She knew she sounded

defiant but she didn't care. 'I've decided. How hard can one dog be? I can do this. Kleppy is mine.'

Fred did his best to dissuade her. 'A dog is for life, Abigail. Small dogs like Kleppy live for sixteen years or longer. That's ten years at least of keeping this dog.'

'Yes.' But ten years? That was a fact to give her pause.

But the paw...

'He's a mutt,' Fred said. 'Mostly Cairn but a bit of something else.'

'That's okay.' Her voice was better, she decided. Firmer. If she was adopting a stray, what use was a pedigree?

'What will Philip say?'

'Philip will say I'm crazy, but it'll be fine,' she said stoutly, though in truth she did have qualms. 'Is he okay?'

Fred was checking him, even as he tried to dissuade her. 'He seems shocked, and he's much thinner than when Isaac brought him in for his last vaccinations. My guess is that he's barely eaten since the old man died. Isaac found him six years back, as a pup, dumped out in the bush. There were a few problems, but in the end they were pretty much inseparable.'

Inseparable? The word suddenly pushed her back to the scene she'd just left. To Raff.

Once upon a time, she and Raff had been inseparable, she thought, and inexplicably there was a crazy twist of her heart.

Inseparable. This dog. The paw...

'He looks okay,' Fred said, feeding him a liver treat. Kleppy took it with dignified politeness. 'Just deflated from what life's done to him. So now what?'

'I take him home.'

'You'll need food. Bedding. A decent chain.'

'I'll stop at the pet store. Tell me what to get.'

But Fred was glancing at his watch, looking anxious. 'I'm urgently needed at a calving. Tell you what, you'll be seeing Raff again in court. Raff'll tell you what you need.'

'How did you know…?'

'Everyone knows everything in Banksia Bay,' Fred said. 'I know where you're supposed to be right now. I know Raff's had the case set back half an hour and I hear Judge Weatherby's not happy. He's fed up with Raff though, not you, so chances are you'll get Baxter off. Which no one in Banksia Bay will be happy about. But hey, if your fees go toward buying dog food, then who am I to argue? Get Baxter off, then talk to Raff about dog food. He gets a discount at the Stock and Station store.'

'Why?'

'Because Raff has one pony, two dogs, three cats, two rabbits and, at last count, eighteen guinea pigs,' Fred said, handing her Kleppy and starting to clear up. 'His place is a menagerie. It's a wonder he didn't take this one but I guess even Raff has limits. He has a lot on his plate. See you later, love. Happy wedding and happy new dog.'

CHAPTER TWO

SHE couldn't go to the Stock and Station store now. That'd have to wait until she'd talked to Raff. Still, Kleppy obviously needed something. What? Best guess.

She stopped at the supermarket and bought a water bowl, a nice red lead with pictures of balls on it and a marrowbone.

She drove to the courthouse and Kleppy lay on the passenger seat and looked anxious. His tail had stopped wagging.

'Hey, I saved you,' she told him. 'Look happy.'

He obviously didn't get the word *saved*. He sort of… hunched.

What was she going to do with him while she was in court?

She drove her car into her personal parking space. How neat was this? She remembered the day her name had gone up. Her parents had cracked champagne.

It was a fine car park. But…it was in full sun.

She might not be a dog person but she wasn't dumb. She couldn't leave Kleppy here. Nor could she take him home—or not yet—not until she'd done something about dog-proofing. Her parents? Ha! They'd take him right back to Fred.

So she drove two blocks to the local park. There were shade trees here and she could tie him by her car. Anyone passing would know he hadn't been abandoned.

She hoped Kleppy would know it, too.

She gave him water and his bone and he slumped on the ground and looked miserable.

Maybe he didn't know it.

She looked at him and sighed. She took off her jacket—her lovely tailored jacket that matched her skirt exactly—and she laid it beside Kleppy.

He sniffed it. The paw came out again—and he inched forward on his belly until it was under him.

Her very expensive jacket was on dirt and grass, and under dog. Her professional jacket.

She didn't actually like that jacket anyway; she preferred less serious clothes. She was five foot four and a bit…mousy. But maybe lawyers should be mousy. Her shiny brown hair curled happily when she let it hang to her shoulders but Philip liked it in a chignon. She had freckles but Philip liked her to wear foundation that disguised them. She had a neat figure that looked good in a suit. Professional. Lawyers should be professional.

She'd given up on *professional* this morning. She was so late.

Oh, but Kleppy looked sad.

'I'll be back at midday,' she told him. 'Two hours, tops. Promise. Then we'll work out where we go from here.'

Where? She'd think of something. She must.

Maybe Raff…

There was a thought.

Fred had said Raff had a menagerie. What difference would one dog make? Once upon a time, he'd had seven.

Instead of advice, maybe she could persuade him to take him.

'You'd like Rafferty Finn,' she told Kleppy. 'He's basically a good man.' Good but flawed—*trouble*—but she didn't need to go into that with Kleppy.

But how to talk him into it? Or Philip into the alternative?

It was too hard to think of that right now. She grabbed her briefcase and headed to the courthouse without looking back. Or without looking back more than half a dozen times.

Kleppy watched her until she was out of sight.

Heart twist. She didn't want to leave him.

It couldn't matter. Her work was in front of her and what was more important than work?

What was facing her was the case of The Crown versus Wallace Baxter.

Wallace was one of three Banksia Bay accountants. The other two made modest incomes. Wallace, however, had the biggest house in Banksia Bay. The Baxter kids went to the best private school in Sydney. Sylvia Baxter drove a Mercedes Coupé, and they skied in Aspen twice a year. They owned a lodge there.

'Lucky investments,' Wallace always said but, after years of juggling, his web of dealings had turned into one appalling tangle. Wallace himself wasn't suffering—his house, cars, even the ski lodge in Aspen, were all in his wife's name—but there were scores of Banksia Bay's retirees who were suffering a lot.

'It's just the financial crisis,' Wallace had said as Philip and Abby had gone over his case notes. 'I can't be responsible for the failure of overseas banks. Just because I'm global...'

Because he was global, his financial dealings were hard to track.

This was a small case by national standards. The Crown Prosecutor who covered Banksia Bay should have retired years ago. The case against Wallace had been left pretty much to Raff, who had few resources and less time. So Raff was right— Philip and Abby had every chance of getting their client off.

Philip rose to meet her, looking relieved. The documents they needed were in her briefcase. He kept the bulk of the confidential files, but it was her job to bring day to day stuff to court.

'What the...?'

'Did Raff tell you what happened?'

Philip cast Raff a look of irritation across the court. There was no love lost between these two men—there never had been. 'He said you had to take a dog to the vet, to get it put down. Isn't that his job?'

'He had cars to move.'

'He got here before you. What kept you? And where's your jacket?'

'It got dog hair on it.' That, at least, was true. 'Can we get on?'

'It'd be appreciated,' the judge said dryly from the bench.

So she sat and watched as Philip decimated the Crown's case. Maybe his irritation gave him an edge this morning, she thought. He was smooth, intelligent, insightful—the best lawyer she knew. He'd do magnificently in the city. That he'd returned home to Banksia Bay—to her—seemed incredible.

Her parents thought so. They loved him to bits. What was more, Philip's father had been her brother Ben's godfather. They were almost family already.

'He almost makes up for our Ben,' her mother said over and over, and their engagement had been a foregone conclusion that made everyone happy.

Except… Except…

Don't go there.

She generally didn't. It was only in the small hours when she woke and thought of Philip's dry kisses, and thought why don't I feel…why don't I feel…?

Like she did when she looked at Rafferty Finn?

No. This was pre-wedding nerves. She had no business thinking like that. If she so much as looked at Raff in that way it'd break her parents' hearts.

So no and no and no.

Raff was on the stand now, steady and sure, giving his evidence with solid backup. His investigation stretched over years, with so many pointers…

But all of those pointers were circumstantial.

She suspected there were things in Philip's briefcase that might not be circumstantial.

Um…don't go there. There was such a thing as lawyer-client confidentiality. Even if Baxter admitted dishonesty to them outright—which he hadn't—they couldn't use it against him.

So Raff didn't have the answers to Philip's questions. The

Crown Prosecutor didn't ask the right questions of Baxter. It'd take a few days, maybe more, but even by lunch time no one doubted the outcome.

At twelve the court rose. The courtroom emptied.

'You might like to go home and get another jacket,' Philip said. 'I'm taking Wallace to lunch.'

She wasn't up to explaining about Kleppy right now. Where to start? But she surely didn't want to have lunch with Wallace. Acting for the guy made her feel dirty.

'Go ahead,' she said.

Philip left, escorting a smug Wallace. She felt an almost irresistible urge to talk to the Crown Prosecutor, tell him to push harder.

It was only suspicion. She had no proof.

'Thanks for taking Kleppy.' Raff was right behind her, and made her jump. Her heart did the same stupid skittering thing it had done for years whenever she heard his voice. She turned to face him and he was smiling at her, looking rueful. 'Sorry, Abby. That was a hard thing to ask you to do this morning, but I had no choice.'

Putting Kleppy down. A hard thing…

'It was too hard,' she whispered. The Crown Prosecutor was leaving for lunch. If she wanted to talk to him…

She was lawyer for the defence. What was she thinking?

'Hey, but you're tough.' Raff motioned to the back of the courtroom, where Bert and Gwen Mackervale were shuffling out to find somewhere to eat their packed sandwiches. 'Not like the Mackervales. They're as soft a touch as any I've seen. They lost their house, yet you'll get Wallace off.'

'Raff, this is inappropriate. I'm a defence lawyer. You know it's what I do.'

'You don't have to. You're better than this, Abby.'

'No, I'm not.'

'Yeah, well…' He shrugged. 'I'm going to find me a hamburger. See you later.'

Uh-oh. Maybe she shouldn't have snapped. Definitely she

shouldn't have snapped. Not when there was such a big favour to ask.

How to ask?

Just ask.

'You couldn't cope with another dog, could you?' she managed and he stilled.

'Another...'

'I couldn't,' she whispered. 'I can't. He's still alive. Raff, he...he looked at me.'

'He looked at you.' Raff was looking at her as if she'd just landed from Mars.

'I couldn't get him put down.'

Raff was carrying papers. He placed them on the nearest bench without breaking his gaze. He stared at her for a full minute.

She didn't stare back. She stared at her shoes instead. They were nice black shoes. Maybe a bit high. Pert, she thought. Pert was good.

There was a smudge on one toe. She considered bending to wipe it and decided against it.

Still silence.

'You're keeping Kleppy?' he said at last.

She shook her head. 'I'm...I don't think it's possible. I'm asking if you could take him. Fred says you have a menagerie. One more wouldn't...wouldn't be much more trouble. I could pay you for his keep.'

'Fred suggested...' He sounded flabbergasted.

'He didn't,' she admitted. 'I thought of it myself.'

'That I'd take Kleppy?'

'Yes,' she whispered and she thought that she sounded about eight years old again. She sounded pathetic.

'No,' he said.

She looked up at him then. Raff Finn was a good six inches taller than she was. More. He was a bit too big. He was a bit too male. He was a bit too...Raff?

He was also a bit too angry.

'N…No?'

'No!' His expression was a mixture of incredulity and fury. 'I don't believe this. You strung out a dog's life in the hope I'd take him?'

'No, I…'

'Do you know how miserable he is?'

'That's why I…'

'Decided to give him to me. Thanks, Abby, but no.'

'But…'

'I'm not a soft option.'

'You have all those animals.'

'Because Sarah loves them. Do you know how much they cost to feed? I can't go away. I can't do anything because Sarah breaks her heart over each and every one of them. Don't you dare do this to me, Abby. I'm not your soft option. If you saved Kleppy, then he's yours.'

'I can't…'

'And neither can I. You brought this on yourself. You deal with it yourself.' His voice was rough as gravel, his anger palpable. 'I need to go. I didn't get breakfast and I don't intend to miss lunch. I'll see you back in court at one.'

He turned away. He strode to the court door and she chewed her lip and thought. But then she decided there wasn't time for thinking. She panicked instead.

'Raff?'

He stopped, not looking back. 'What?'

Sometimes only an apology would do. She was smart enough to know that this was one of those times. Maybe a little backtracking wouldn't hurt either.

'Raff, I'm very sorry,' she said. 'It was just a thought—or maybe it was just a wild hope—but the decision to save Kleppy was mine. Asking you was an easy option and I won't ask again. But, moving on, if I'm to keep him… I know nothing about dogs. Fred didn't suggest you take him, but he did suggest I ask you for help. He said you'll tell me all the things I need to care for him. So please…'

'Please what?'

'Just tell me what I need to buy at the Stock and Station store. I have a meeting with the wedding caterers after work, so I need to do my shopping now.'

'You're seriously thinking you'll keep him?'

'I don't have a choice.'

He was facing her now, his face a mixture of incredulity and…laughter? Where had laughter come from? 'You're keeping *Kleppy?*' He said it as if she'd chosen Kleppy above all others.

'There's no other dogs out there?' she said, alarmed, and he grinned. His grin lit his face—lit the whole court. Oh, she knew that grin…

Trouble. Tragedy.

'There's thousands of dogs,' he said. 'So many needing homes. But you have to fall for Kleppy.'

'What's wrong with Kleppy?'

'Nothing.' He was still grinning. 'I take it you haven't told Philip.'

'I… No.'

'So where's Kleppy now?' His grin faded. 'You haven't left him in the car? The sun…'

'I know that much,' she said, indignant. 'I took the car to the park and I tied him to a nice shady tree. He has water and feed. He even has my jacket.'

'He has your jacket.' He sounded bemused, as if there was some private joke she wasn't privy to.

'Yes.'

'And you've tied him up…how?'

'I bought a lead.'

'Please tell me it's a chain.'

'The chains looked cruel. It's webbing. Pretty. Red with pictures of balls on it.'

'I don't believe this.'

'What's wrong?'

But she didn't have a chance to answer. Instead, he grabbed

her hand, towed her out of the courthouse—practically at a run—and he headed for the park.

Dragging her behind him.

Kleppy was gone.

Her pretty red lead was chewed into two pieces—or at least she assumed it was chewed into two pieces. One piece was still tied to the tree.

Her jacket lay on the ground, rumpled. The water bowl was half empty. Apparently chewing leads was thirsty work. The marrowbone wasn't touched.

No dog.

'He doesn't like being confined, our Kleppy,' Raff said, taking in the scene with professional care.

'You know this how?' *He'd chewed through a lead?*

'It's always been a problem. I'm guessing he'll make tracks up to the Abrahams place, but who knows where he'll end up in the meantime.'

'He'll be up at Isaac's?'

Isaac lived halfway up the mountain at the back of the town. Raff was looking concerned. 'It is a bit far,' he admitted. 'And from here... It'll be off his chosen beat.' He raked his hair. 'Of all the stupid... I don't have time to go look for a dog.'

'I'll look for him.'

'You know where to look?'

'Do you?'

'Backyards,' he said. 'Never takes the fastest route, our Kleppy.' He raked his hair again. Looking tired. 'I need lunch. If I'm not back in court at one then Baxter'll definitely get off. You need to do this, Abby. I can't.'

Look for a dog all afternoon... 'Philip'll kill me.'

'Then I guess the wedding'll be off. Is that a good thing?'

Raff spoke absently, as if it didn't bother him if her wedding was at risk. As indeed it didn't. What business was it of his to care about the wedding? What business was it of his to even comment on it? She opened her mouth to say so, but suddenly his gaze focused, sharpened. 'Is that...?'

She turned to see.

It was—and the change was extraordinary.

When she'd left him two hours ago, Kleppy had looked defeated and depressed. When he'd crawled onto her jacket he hadn't had the energy to even rise off his stomach.

Now he was prancing across the park towards them, looking practically jaunty. His rough coat was never going to be pretty. One of his ears flopped down, almost covering his eye. His tail was a bit ragged.

But they could see his tail wagging when he was still a hundred yards away. And, as he got closer…

He had something in his mouth. Something pink and lacy. What the…?

'It's a bra,' Abby breathed as the little dog reached them. She bent down and the dog circled her twice, then came to her outstretched hand. He rubbed himself against her leg and his whole body shivered. With delight?

He was carrying the bra like a trophy. She touched it and he dropped it into her hand, then stood back as if he'd just presented her with a cheque for a million dollars. His body language was unmistakable.

Look what I've found for you! Aren't I the cleverest dog in the world?

She dropped the bra and picked him up, hugging him close. He wriggled frantically and she put him back down. He picked up the bra again, placed it back in her hand and then allowed her to pick him up—as long as she kept the bra.

His meaning couldn't be plainer. 'I've brought you a gift. You appreciate it.'

'You've brought me a bra,' she managed and she felt like crying. 'Oh, Kleppy…'

'It could just as easily have been men's jocks,' Raff said. He lifted the end of the bra that was hanging loose. There was a price tag attached. 'I thought so. He's a bit small to rob clothes lines, our Kleppy. This has come from Main Street. Morrisy Drapers are having a sale. This will have come from the discount bin at the front of the store.'

Had it? She checked it out. Cop and lawyer for the defence, standing in the sun, examining evidence.

Pink bra. Nylon. White and silver frills. About an E Plus Cup. Room for about three of Abby.

'Very…very useful,' Abby managed.

'You'll need to pay for it.'

'Sorry?'

'It's theft,' Raff said, touching the bra's middle with a certain degree of caution. It was looking a bit soggy. 'He never hurts anything. He hunts treasures; he never destroys them. But they do get a bit…wet. Taking it back and apologising's not going to cut it.'

'Will they know he's stolen it?'

'He's not a cat burglar,' Raff said gravely, though the sides of his mouth were twitching. 'Dog burglars don't have the same finesse. He's a snatch and grab man, our Kleppy. There'll be a dozen people on Main Street who'll be able to identify him in a line up.'

'Oh, my…' And then she paused. Kleppy.

Kleppy was a strange name but she'd hardly had time to think about it. Now… 'Kleppy. Oh…'

Raff looked like a man starting to enjoy himself. 'Got it,' he said, grinning. 'And there's another reason you're not offloading this mutt onto me. This is a dog who lives to present his master with surprises. No dead rats or old bones for his guy. It has to be interesting. Expensive is good. One of a set's his favourite. Isaac gave up on him long since—he just paid for the damage and got on with it. So now here's Kleppy, deciding you're his new owner. Welcome to dog ownership, Abigail Callahan. You're the proud owner of Banksia Bay's biggest kleptomaniac—and also the littlest.'

A kleptomaniac… Kleppy.

She stared at Raff as if he was out of his mind. He gazed back, lips twitching, that dangerous smile lurking deep within.

She was about to present her fiancé with a kleptomaniac dog?

'I don't believe it,' she managed at last. 'There's no such thing.'

'You want to know how I know this dog?' He wasn't even trying to disguise his grin. 'I'd like to say I'm personally acquainted with every dog in Banksia Bay but, even with Sarah's help, I can't manage that. Nope, I'm acquainted with Kleppy because I've arrested him.'

'Arrested…'

'I've caught him red-handed—or red-pawed—on any number of occasions. The problem is that he doesn't know how to hide it. Like now. He steals and then he shows off.'

'I don't believe it.'

'You've already said that.'

'But…'

'That's why no one wants him,' he said, humour fading. 'He's always been a problem. Henrietta's had to be honest with everyone who came to the Shelter looking for the ideal pet. He isn't ideal. Isaac paid out on Kleppy's behalf more times than I can say. He's hidden stuff and he's been accused of stealing himself. Isaac never cared what people thought of him, which was just as well, as there's been more women's underwear end up at his house than you can imagine. He burned most of it— what choice did he have? Can you imagine wandering the town saying who owns this G-string? But he loved Kleppy, you see.' The smile returned. 'Like you will.'

'I… This is appalling.'

'I told you to get him put down.'

'You know I'm a soft option.' Anger hit then, fury, pure and simple. 'You know me, Raff Finn. You put this dog in my car because you knew I wouldn't be able to have him put down. You know I'm a soft touch.'

'Now how would I know that?' he said softly. 'I haven't known you for a very long time, Abby. You've grown up. You've got yourself engaged to Philip. The Abby I knew could no sooner have married Philip than fly. You're a lawyer engaged in getting Wallace Baxter off. A lawyer doing cases like that—of course you can get a dog put down.'

His gaze met hers, direct, challenging, knowing he was calling a bluff she couldn't possibly meet.

'You still can,' he told her. 'Put Kleppy in the car and take him back to Fred. You've made his last hours happy by giving him the freedom for one last hoist. He'll die a happy dog.'

You still can.

Say something.

She couldn't think of a thing to say.

She was hugging Kleppy, who had a pink bra somehow looped around his ears.

She still hugged Kleppy.

What Raff was saying was sensible. Very sensible. There were too many dogs in the world. She'd done her best by this one. She'd let him have a happy morning—if indeed Raff was right and Kleppy did enjoy stealing.

But he was certainly a happier dog now than he'd been when she'd first met him. He was warm and nuzzly. He was poking his damp nose against her neck, giving her a tentative lick.

His backside was wriggling.

Take him back to Fred? No way.

She'd always wanted a dog.

Philip would hate a dog.

Her marriage suddenly loomed before her. Loomed? Wrong word, but she couldn't think of another one.

Philip was wonderful. He was her rock. He'd looked after her and her family for ever. When Ben had died he'd held her up when her world seemed to be disintegrating.

Philip was right for her. Her parents loved him. Everyone thought Philip was wonderful. If she hadn't married him...

She *hadn't* married him, she reminded herself. Not yet. That was the point.

In nine days she'd be married. She'd move into the fabulous house Philip had bought for them, and she'd be Philip's wife.

Philip's wife would never bring home a kleptomaniac dog. She'd never bring home any sort of dog. So, if she wanted one...

She took a deep breath and she knew exactly what she'd do. Her last stand… Like it or leave it, she thought, and she sounded desperate, even to herself. But she had made up her mind.

'I'm keeping him.'

'Good for you,' Raff said and the twinkle was back with a vengeance. 'Can I be there when you tell Philip?'

'Get lost.'

'That's not kind. Not when you need help to buy what Kleppy needs.'

'I'm starting to get a very good idea of what Kleppy needs,' she said darkly. 'An eight-foot fence and a six-foot chain.'

'He'll mope.'

'Then he'll have to learn not to mope. It's that or dead.'

'You'll explain that to him how?'

'You're not being helpful.'

'No,' he said and glanced at his watch. 'I'm not. I need a hamburger and time's running out before court resumes. You want a list?'

'No. I mean…' The afternoon suddenly stretched before her, long and lonely. Or not long and lonely for her. Long and lonely for the little dog squirming in her arms. Her thief. 'I do need a list. I also need a chain.' She hesitated. 'But I can't leave him here. This morning was only two hours. This afternoon's four at least before I can collect him.'

'So take him home.'

'I can't.' It was practically a wail. She caught herself. Fought for a little dignity. 'I mean…it's not dog-proof. I need an hour or so there to get things organised.'

'That's fair enough.' He paused, surveyed her face and then decided to be helpful. 'You want me to ask Sarah to help?'

Sarah. Her eyes widened. Of course. Sarah loved dogs. And… Maybe her first suggestion was still possible. Maybe…

'No,' Raff said before she opened her mouth. 'Sarah's not taking ownership of another dog and if you ask her I'll personally run you out of town. I mean that, Abby.'

'I wouldn't ask her.'

'No?'

She managed a twisted smile, abandoning her last forlorn hope.

'No.'

'Good, then,' he said briskly, moving on. 'But she'll enjoy taking care of him this afternoon. Kleppy'll be tired after his excursion. We have a safe yard. The other dogs are quiet—they won't overwhelm him—and you can come by this evening and pick him up.'

Go back to Raff's? She couldn't imagine doing that. But Raff was moving on.

'It's a good offer,' Raff said. 'Take it or leave it, but do it now. If you accept, then I'll lock this convicted thief in my patrol car and take him out to Sarah. I may even do it with lights and sirens if it means getting back to court on time. You can take my list and go buy what you need and get back to court on time as well. Or I leave you to it. What's it to be, Abby?'

'I…' She was starting to panic. Go out to Raff's tonight? To Raff's? She hadn't been there since…

'Unless you have another friend you can call on?' he suggested, and maybe her emotions were on her face. Definitely her emotions were on her face.

'All my friends work,' she wailed.

'Then it's Sarah. Tonight, and you *will* collect him.' That irrepressible grin emerged again. 'Hey, you have a dog. What a wedding gift. To you and to Philip, one kleptomaniac dog. Happy wedding.'

He drove out to Sarah with Kleppy beside him and he found the smile inside him growing. Somewhere inside, the Abby he'd once known and loved was still there.

Once upon a time she'd loved him.

That had been years ago. A teenage romance. Yes, they'd felt as if they were truly, madly, deeply, but they were only kids.

At nineteen he'd headed off to Sydney to Police Training College. Abby had been stuck in Banksia Bay until she finished school, and she'd needed a partner for her debutante ball.

He still remembered the arguments. 'You're my boyfriend. How can I have anyone else as my partner? Why can't you come home more often so we can practice?'

And more… 'You and Ben are totally obsessed with that car. Every time you come home, that's all you ever think about.'

They were kids. He hadn't seen her need, and she hadn't seen his. Philip had been home from university; he'd agreed to partner her for her ball and Raff was given the cold shoulder.

They'd been kids moving on. Changing.

They had changed, he conceded, only just now he'd seen a glimpse that the old Abby was still in there. Feisty and funny and gorgeous.

But still…unforgiving, and who could blame her?

He'd forgiven himself. He didn't need Abigail Callahan's forgiveness. He couldn't need it.

If only she wasn't adorable.

CHAPTER THREE

THE afternoon was interminable. The case was boring—financial evidence that was as dry as dust.

The courtroom was as dry as dust.

She couldn't think of a way to tell Philip.

All afternoon she was aware of Raff on the opposite side of the courtroom. He was here this afternoon to present the police case. Thankfully, he wouldn't be here for the rest of the week. He was called away twice, for which she was also thankful, but he wasn't called away for long enough.

He was watching her.

He was waiting for her to tell Philip?

He was laughing at her. She knew he was. The man spelled trouble and he'd just got her into more.

Trouble? One small dog, easily contained in a secure backyard. How hard could this be?

So tell Philip.

There was lots of time. The police case went on for most of the afternoon—tedious financial details. She and Philip both knew it back to front. There were gaps while documents were given to the jury. She had time to tell him.

Philip would be civilised about it. He'd never raise his voice to her, especially not in a courtroom. But still…

She couldn't.

Across the court, Raff still watched her.

Finally the court rose. Raff crossed the courtroom and Abby panicked. *Don't say anything.*

'You guys okay?' he asked, and anyone who didn't know him would think it was simply a courtesy question. They wouldn't see that lurking laughter. *Trouble.*

'Why wouldn't we be?' Philip demanded, irritated. He disliked Raff—of course he did. He showed no outright aggression—simply cool, professional interaction and nothing more.

'It's getting close to your wedding,' Raff said. 'No last minute nerves? No last minute hitches?'

'We need to go,' Abby said, feeling close to hysterics. 'I have a meeting with the caterers in half an hour.'

'I bet there's lots of stuff you need to do.' Raff's voice was sympathy itself. 'Messy things, weddings.'

'Not ours,' Philip snapped. 'Everything's under control. Isn't that right, sweetheart?'

'I…yes.' Just go away, Raff. Get out of our lives. 'Are you coming to the caterers with me, Philip?'

'I can't.' Philip turned a shoulder on Raff, excluding him completely. 'My dad and my uncles are taking me out to dinner and bowling. A boys only night. I thought I told you.'

He had.

'That sounds exciting,' Raff said, mildly interested. 'Bowling, huh. I guess I won't be untying you naked from in front of the Country Women's Association clubrooms at dawn, then.'

'My friends…'

'Don't do wild buck's nights,' Raff said approvingly. 'I guessed that. You'll probably be home in bed by eight. So you're alone tonight, Abby? Organising caterers on your lonesome. And anything else you need to do.'

'Could you please…' she started and then stopped, the impossibility of asking another favour—asking him to bring Kleppy home—overwhelming her.

'Nope,' Raff said. 'Not if you're about to ask me anything that involves the wedding. Me and weddings keep far away from each other.'

'We're not asking you to be involved,' Philip snapped. 'Abby can cope with the caterers herself. Ready to go, sweetheart?'

'Yes,' she managed and allowed Philip to usher her out of the court.

She should have told Philip then. She had ten minutes while Philip went over the results of the day, what they needed to do to strengthen their case the next morning, a few wedding details he'd forgotten to cover.

Philip was a man at ease with himself. It was only when Raff was around that he got prickly and maybe…well, that did have to do with their past. Raff had messed with Philip's life as well as hers.

Philip was a good man. He was looking forward to his wedding. His father and his uncles were taking him out for a pre-wedding night with the boys and he'd enjoy it.

She didn't want to mess with that until she must, even if it did mean delaying telling him about Kleppy; even if it meant going to Raff's alone. Maybe it'd be better going alone. Going with Philip… It could make things worse.

'Come round tonight after bowling,' she told him, kissing him lightly on the lips. Her fiancé. Her husband in nine days. She loved him.

And if he was a bit dull… He'd had his days of being wild, they all had, before life had taught them that caution was good.

'We should get a good night's sleep,' he said.

'Yes, but there are things we need to discuss.' He'd like Kleppy when he saw him, she decided. Kleppy of the limpid eyes, wide and brown and innocent.

She should change his name. To Rover? Rover was a Philipish name for a dog.

But Kleppy suited him.

'What do we need to discuss?' he was asking.

Say it.

No. Introduce him to Kleppy as a done deal.

'Just…caterers and things. I don't want to make too many decisions on my own.'

He smiled and kissed her and she had to stop herself from thinking dry and dusty. 'You need to have more self-confidence. Make your own decisions. You're a big girl now.'

'I...yes.'

'Anything you decide is fine by me.'

'But you will drop by?'

'I'll drop by. Night, sweetheart.' And off he went for his night with the boys. His dad and his uncles. Bowling. Yeeha!

And that was the type of thinking that was getting her into trouble, she decided. So cut it out.

Philip was a lovely man. He was handsome. He was beautifully groomed. They'd had a very nice holiday last year—they'd gone to Italy and Philip had had four suits made there. They were lovely suits. He'd also had two briefcases made—matching ones, magnificent leather, discreetly initialled and fitted out to Philip's specifications. She'd only been mildly irritated when he'd decreed—for the sake of the briefcases—her surname would be his.

What was the issue, after all? She was to be his wife.

But buying suits and briefcases had taken almost half of their holiday.

Cut it out!

It was just... Raff had unsettled her. This whole day had unsettled her.

'So go home and organise your house for one small dog, then go organise caterers,' she told herself. 'Oh, and pay for Kleppy's stolen goods. Just do what has to be done, one step at a time.'

And then go out to Raff's?

Aargh.

She could do this.

She could visit Rafferty Finn.

She could do it. One step at a time.

The rest of the afternoon was full, but Abby and her dog were front and centre of his thoughts. He shouldn't have offered to bring Kleppy home. Not this afternoon. Not ever.

He didn't want her coming here.

After dinner, Raff washed and Sarah wiped, while Sarah told him about her day, the highlight of which had been minding Kleppy.

'He's a sweetheart,' his sister told him, her face softening at the thought of the little dog. 'He's so cuddly. Why does he love his bra?'

'He's a thief. He likes stealing things. He's a bad dog.' He found himself smiling at the thought of strait-laced Abigail Callahan having to front up and pay for stolen goods.

Maybe it wasn't a good idea to keep thinking of Abby. Not like this.

She was Philip's fiancée. Anything between them was a distant memory. It had to be.

But Sarah was looking doubtful. She looked down at Kleppy, snoozing by the fire, his bra tucked underneath him. 'He doesn't look bad. He's really cute and Abby's very busy. Are you sure Abby wants him?'

Raff hardened his heart. 'I'm sure.'

'And Abby's coming tonight?'

'Yes.'

'Abby's my friend.'

She was. The tension of the day lessened a little at that. No matter what lay between Raff and Abby, no matter how much she hated seeing him, Abby had always been Sarah's friend.

They'd all been best friends at the time of the accident. Ben and Raff. Abby and Sarah. Two big brothers, two little sisters. Philip had been in there, too. A gang of five.

But one car crash and friendship had been blown to bits.

In the months that followed, no matter that Abby had loathed Raff so much that seeing him made her cry, she'd stuck by Sarah. She'd visited her in Sydney, despite her parents' disapproval, taking the train week after week to Sydney Central Hospital and then later to the rehabilitation unit on North Shore.

Back home, Sarah's friends had fallen away. Acquired brain injury was a hard thing for friends to handle. Sarah was still

Sarah, and yet not. She'd struggled with everything—relearning speaking, walking, the simplest of survival skills.

They'd come so far. She could now almost live independently—almost, but not quite. She had her animals and their little farm Raff kept for her. She worked in the local sheltered workshop three days a week, and twice a week Abby met her after work for drinks.

Drinks being milkshakes. Two friends, catching up on their news.

Raff would pick Sarah up and she'd be happy, bubbly about going out with her friend—but Abby would always have slipped away from the café just before Raff was due. Since the accident, Abby had never come back to their farm. She'd never talked to Raff unless she absolutely must, but she'd never taken that anger out on Sarah.

'I'm glad Abby's coming tonight,' Sarah said simply. 'And I'm glad she's getting a dog. Abby's lonely.'

Lonely? Sarah rarely had insights. This one was startling. 'No, she's not. She's getting married to Philip.'

'I don't like Philip,' Sarah said.

That was unusual, too. Sarah liked everyone. When Philip met her—as of course he did because this wasn't a big town— he was unfailingly friendly. But still… In the times when Raff had been with her and they'd met Philip, Sarah's hand had crept to his and she'd clung.

Was that from memories of the accident?

The accident. Don't go there.

'There's nothing wrong with Philip,' he told Sarah.

'I want Abby to come,' Sarah said, wiping her last pot with a fierceness unusual for her. 'But I don't want Philip. He makes me scared.'

Scared?

'The man's boring,' Raff said. 'There's nothing to be scared about.'

'I just don't like him,' Sarah said and, logical or not, Raff felt exactly the same.

* * *

She didn't want to go.

She must.

She gazed round her little house with a carefully appraising eye. She'd hung her wedding dress in the spare room and she'd packed away everything else she thought a dog might hurt.

She'd bought a dog kennel for outside and a basket for inside.

She'd bought a chain for emergencies but she didn't intend using it. Her back garden was enclosed with a four-foot brick fence, and she'd checked and rechecked for gaps.

She had dog food, dog shampoo, flea powder, worm pills, a dog brush, padding for his kennel and a book on training your dog. She'd had a quick browse through the book. There was nothing about kleptomania, but confinement would fix that.

She'd take him for a long walk every day. Kleppy might sometimes be lonely, she conceded, but surely loneliness was better than the fate that had been waiting for him.

And if he was lonely… She might sneak him into the office occasionally.

That, though, was for the future. For now, she was ready to fetch him. From Raff.

So fetch him. There's not a lot of use staring at preparations, she told herself. It's time to go claim your dog.

It was eight o'clock. Philip's night out would be over by ten and she had to be back here by then.

Of course she'd be back. Ten minutes drive out. Two minutes to collect Kleppy and say hi to Sarah. Ten minutes back.

Just go.

She hadn't been out there since…

Just go.

'When will she be here?'

'Any time soon.'

He shouldn't care. He shouldn't even be here. There was bound to be something cop-like that needed his attention at the station—only that might look like he was running, and Rafferty Finn wasn't a man who ran.

'She never comes here.'

'She likes going to cafés with you too much.'

Sarah giggled, hugging Kleppy close. This place was pretty relaxed for a dog. The screen door stayed permanently open and the dogs wandered in and out at will. The gate to the back garden was closed, but Kleppy seemed content to be hugged by Sarah, to watch television and to occasionally eat popcorn.

Raff watched television, too. Or sort of. It was hard to watch when every sense was tuned to a car arriving.

The Finn place hadn't changed.

The moon was full but she hardly needed to see. She'd come here so often, to the base of Black Mountain, that she knew every bend. As kids, she and Ben had ridden their bikes here almost every day.

This had been their magic place.

Her parents had disapproved. 'The Finns,' her mother had told them over and over, 'are not our sort of people.' By that she meant they didn't fit into her social mould.

Abby and Ben didn't care.

Old Mrs Finn—everybody called her Gran—had been the family's stability. Gran's husband had died long before Abby had known her, and it was rumoured that his death had been a relief, for the town as well as for Gran. After his death, Gran had quietly got on with life. She ran a few sheep, a few pigs, a lot of poultry. Her garden was amazing. She seemed to spend her life in the kitchen and her baking was wonderful.

Abby barely remembered Raff and Sarah's mother, but there had been disapproving whispers about her as well. She'd run away from home at fifteen, then come home unwed with two small children.

She'd worked in the local supermarket for a time. Abby had vague memories of a silent woman with haunted eyes, with none of the life and laughter of her mother or her children.

She'd died when Abby was about seven. Abby remembered little fuss, just a family who'd got on with it. Gran had taken over her grandchildren's care. Life had gone on and the Finns were still disapproved of.

Abby and Ben had loved it here. They had always been welcome.

And now? She turned into the drive but her foot eased from the accelerator.

'You're always welcome.' She could remember Gran saying it to her, over and over. She remembered Gran saying it to her after Ben's death. As if she could come back here…

She had come back. Tonight.

This is only about a dog, she told herself, breathing deeply. *Nothing else. The past is gone. There's no use regretting—no use even thinking about it. Go get your dog from Raff Finn and then get off his land.*

Raff never meant…

I know he didn't, she told herself. Of course he didn't. Accidents happened and it was only stupidity.

Could she forgive stupidity?

Ben was dead. Why would she want to?

He saw her stop at the gate. It was after eight—would Philip have finished his wild night out? Would she have him with her?

Maybe that was why they'd stopped. Philip would be doing his utmost to stop her keeping Kleppy.

Would she defy him? She'd need strength if she was going to stay married to Philip. She'd need strength not to be Philip's doormat.

But the thought of Abby as a doormat made him smile. She'd never been a doormat. Abby Callahan was smart, sexy, sassy—and so much more. Or…she had been.

She'd followed him round like a shadow for years. He and Ben had scoffed at Abby and Sarah, the little sisters. They'd teased them, and had given them such a hard time. They'd loved them both. Until…

Until one stupid night. One stupid moment.

He closed his eyes as he'd done so many times. Searching for a memory.

Summer. Nineteen years old. Home from Police Training College. Ben home from university. They'd spent weekend after weekend tinkering with a car they were trying to restore. Finally they'd got it started, towards dusk on the day they were both due to go back to the city. They were pumped with excitement. Aching to see it go.

They couldn't take it on the road—it wasn't registered—but up on Black Mountain, just behind Isaac Abrahams place, there was a cleared firebreak, smoothed for access for fire trucks.

If they could get it out there, they could put it through its paces.

He remembered loading the car on the trailer behind Gran's ancient truck, Ben's dad watching them in disapproval. 'You should be home tonight, Ben. Your mother's expecting you.'

'We need to see this working,' Ben had told him and Mr Callahan had left in a huff.

Sarah was watching them, wistful. 'Can I come?'

'There's not enough room in the truck.'

'What if Philip brings me?'

'Sure. Bring Abby.'

'You know Abby's mad at you—and she's not talking to Philip, either.'

But neither Ben nor Raff were interested. They were only interested in getting their car going.

And it worked. Up on the mountain, he remembered Ben driving, yahooing, both of them high as kites. Months of work paying off.

He remembered getting out. Swapping drivers. Thinking it was too dark to be on this track, and it was starting to rain. Plus Ben had to get back to have dinner with his parents.

But Ben saying, 'We have lights. If I can cope with Mum being fed up, you can cope with a bit of rain. Just do one turn to see for yourself how well she handles.'

Then…nothing. He'd woken in hospital. Concussion. Multiple lacerations. Broken wrist and broken ankle.

All he knew of the accident was what was written in the official reports.

Philip had driven Sarah onto the track to find them. He'd turned off the main road onto the firebreak, and ventured just far enough down the break to reach the crest…

Philip had been the only one uninjured. His recall was perfect, stark and bleak.

Raff had burst over the crest on the wrong side of the road, driving so fast he was almost airborne. Philip had nowhere to go. Both drivers swerved, but not fast enough.

Both cars had ended up in the trees. The rain and the mess from the emergency vehicles had washed the tracks away before the authorities could corroborate Philip's story. Raff couldn't be prosecuted—but he had punishment enough. He'd killed his best mate and he'd destroyed his sister. He missed Ben like he'd miss a twin—an aching, gut-destroying loss. He'd lost a part of Sarah that could never be restored.

His grandmother had died six months later.

And Abby?

Facing Abby had been the hardest thing he'd had to do in his life. The first time he'd seen her…she'd looked at him and it was as if he was some sort of black hole where her heart used to be.

'I'm sorry,' he'd said and she'd simply turned away. She'd stayed away for ten years.

Her brother was dead and sometimes Raff wished it could have been him.

Which was dumb. Who'd take care of Sarah, then?

Let it go.

Go greet Abby. And Philip?

Abby and Philip. Banksia Bay's perfect couple.

CHAPTER FOUR

RAFF was waiting on the veranda and Abby felt her breath catch in her throat. She came close to heading straight back down the mountain.

What was it with this man? She was well over her childhood crush. She'd decided today that it was the uniform making him sexy, but he wasn't wearing a uniform now.

He was in faded jeans and an old T-shirt, stretched a bit tight.

He looked good enough to...

To get away from fast.

He was leaning idly against the veranda post, big, loose-limbed, absurdly good-looking. He was standing with crossed arms, watching her walk towards him. Simply watching.

His eyes said caution.

She didn't need the message. Caution? She had it in spades.

'Where's Kleppy?' she asked, and she knew she sounded snappy but there wasn't a thing she could do about it.

'Phil's still on his wild night out?'

'Cut it out, Raff.'

'Sorry,' he said. Then he hesitated and his eyes narrowed. 'Nope. Come to think of it, I'm not sorry. Why are you marrying that stuffed shirt?'

'Don't be insulting.'

'He's wealthy,' Raff conceded. 'Parents own half Banksia Bay. He's making a nice little income himself. Or a big income.

He's already bought the dream home. He's starting to look almost as wealthy as Baxter. You guys will be set for life.'

'Stop it,' she snapped. 'Just because he's a responsible citizen...'

'I'm responsible now. Maybe even more responsible than you. What have you got on Baxter that I don't know about?'

'You think Philip and I would ever do anything illegal?'

'Maybe not you. Philip, though...'

'I don't believe this. Of all the... I could sue. Give me my dog.'

'Sarah has your dog,' he said and stood aside, giving her no choice but to enter a house she'd vowed never to set foot in again.

He was standing on the top step of the veranda. He didn't move.

She would not let him make her feel like this. Like she'd felt as a kid.

But her arm brushed his as she passed him, so slightly that with anyone else she wouldn't have noticed.

She noticed. Her arm jerked as if she'd been burned. She glowered and stomped past and still he didn't move.

She pushed the screen door wide and let it bang behind her. She always had. It banged like it always banged and she got the same effect... From the depths of the house came the sound of hysterical barking. She braced.

When she'd been a kid and she'd come here, the Finns' dog pack would knock her over. She'd loved it. She'd be lying in the hall being licked all over, squirming and wriggling, a tadpole in a dog pond, giggling and giggling until Raff hauled the dogs off.

When she didn't end up knocked over she'd felt almost disappointed.

She was bigger now, she conceded. Not so likely to be knocked over by a pack of dogs.

But there weren't as many dogs, anyway. There was an ancient black Labrador, almost grey with age. There was a pug, and there was Kleppy bringing up the rear. Wagging his tail. Greeting her?

She knelt and hugged Kleppy. He licked her face. So did the old Labrador. The pug was young but this one…she even remembered the feel of his tongue. 'Boris!'

'Abby!' Sarah burst out of the kitchen, her beam wide enough to split her face. She dived down onto the floor and hugged her friend with total lack of self-consciousness. 'Abby, you're here. I've made you honey jumbles.'

'I…great.' Maybe she should get up. Lawyer on floor hugging dog…

Boris was licking her chin.

'Boris?' she said tentatively and she included him in the hug she was giving Kleppy.

'He is Boris,' Raff said and she twisted and found Raff was watching them all from the doorway. 'How old was he when you were last here, Abby?'

'I… Three?'

'He's fourteen now. Old for a Labrador. You've missed out on his whole life.'

'That's not all I've missed out on,' she whispered. 'How could I ever come back?' She shook her head and hauled herself to her feet. Raff made an instinctive move to help, but then pulled away. Shook his head. Closed down.

'But you will stay for a bit,' Sarah said, grabbing Abby's hand to pull herself up. Movement was still awkward for Sarah; it always would be. 'I've told the dogs they can have a honey jumble each,' she told Abby. 'But they need to wait until they've cooled down. You can't take Kleppy home before he's had his.'

'I could take it with me.'

'Abby,' Sarah said in a term of such reproach that Abby knew she was stuck.

How long did honey jumbles take to cool?

Apparently a while because, 'I've just put them in the oven,' Sarah said happily. 'I made a lot after tea but Raff forgot to tell me to take them out. They went black. Even the dogs didn't want them. Raff never forgets,' she said, heading back to the kitchen. 'But he's funny tonight. Do you think it's because you're here?'

'I expect that's it,' Abby said, trying desperately to find something to say. Babbling because of it? 'Maybe it's because I'm a lawyer. Sometimes police don't like lawyers 'cos they ask too many questions.'

'And sometimes they don't ask enough,' Raff growled.

'Meaning…'

'Baxter…'

Oh, for heaven's sake… 'Leave it, Raff,' she said. 'Just butt out of my life.'

'I did that years ago.'

'Well, don't stop now.' She took a deep breath. 'Sarah, love, I'm in a rush.'

'I know you are,' Sarah said and pushed her into a kitchen chair. 'You sit down. Raff will make you a nice cup of tea and we'll talk until the honey jumbles are ready. But don't yell at Raff,' she said disapprovingly. 'Raff's nice.'

Raff was nice? Okay, maybe a part of him was nice. She might want to hate Raff Finn—and a part of her couldn't help but hate him—but she had to concede he was caring for Sarah beautifully.

The twelve months after the crash had been appalling. Even her grief for Ben hadn't stopped Abby seeing the tragedy that was Sarah.

She'd lain unconscious for three weeks and everyone had mourned her as dead. At one time rumour had it that Raff and Gran were asked to stop life support.

At three weeks she'd woken, but it was a different Sarah.

She'd had to relearn everything. Her memory of childhood was patchy. Her recent memory was lost completely.

She'd learned to walk again, to talk. She coped now but her speech was slow, as was her movement. Gran and Raff had brought her home and worked with her, loved her, massaged, exercised, pleaded, cajoled, bullied…

When Gran died Raff had taken it on himself to keep on going. For over a year he hadn't been able to work. They'd lived on the smell of an oily rag, because, 'She's not going into care.'

With anyone else the community would have rallied, but not with the Finns. Not when Raff was seen as being the cause of so much tragedy.

How he'd managed…

If the accident happened now the community would help, she thought. Somehow, in the last years, Raff had redeemed himself. He was a fine cop. He'd cared for Sarah with such love and compassion that the worst of the nay-sayers had been silenced. She'd even thought…it was time she moved on. Time she learned to forgive.

But over and over… He'd killed Ben.

How could she ever be friends with him again?

She didn't need to be. She simply chose to be distant. So she sat in Raff's kitchen while Sarah chatted happily, showing her the guinea pigs, explaining they'd had too many babies and that Raff had told her they had to sell some but how could she choose?

Smelling honey jumbles in a kitchen she loved.

Knowing Raff was watching her.

She found her fingers were clenched on her knees. They were hidden by the table. She could clench them as much as she wanted.

It didn't help. This place was almost claustrophobic, the memories it evoked.

But Raff was watching her and how Raff was making her feel wasn't a memory. This was no childhood crush. It was like a wave of testosterone blasting across the table, assaulting her from every angle.

Sarah was laughing.

Raff wasn't laughing. He was simply watchful.

Judgemental? Because she was marrying Philip?

Why shouldn't she marry Philip? He was kind, thoughtful, clever.

Her fallback?

Um…no. He was her careful choice.

She'd gone out with Philip before Ben had died, just for a bit, when the boys had left home, Raff to the Police Training College, Ben to university.

Philip had left for university, too, but he'd caught glandular fever and come home for a term.

She'd needed a date for her debutante ball and was fed up with Raff being away, with the boys being obsessed with their junk-pile car when they did come home.

Philip had the most wonderful set of wheels. He had money even then. But he wasn't Raff.

She'd made her debut and she'd found an excuse to break up. The decision wasn't met with regret. Philip had immediately asked Sarah out.

Maybe if the accident hadn't happened… Maybe Sarah and Philip…

Where was she going? Don't even think it, she decided. They were different people now.

Philip especially was different. After the crash…he was so caring. Whenever she needed him, he was there. He'd encouraged her to take up law as well. 'You can do it,' he'd said. 'You're bright, organised, meticulous. Do law and we'll set up the best law firm Banksia Bay's ever seen. We can care for our parents that way, Abby. Your parents miss Ben so much. We can be there for them.'

And so they were. It was all working out. All she needed to do was avoid the judgement on Raff's face. And avoid the way Raff made her…feel.

How could he bear her here?

One night, one car crash.

And it stood between him and this woman for ever.

How could she marry Philip?

But he knew. It was even reasonable, he conceded.

Philip was okay. Once he'd even been a friend. Yes, the man made money and Raff did wonder how, but that was just his nasty cop mind. Yes, he took on cases Raff wouldn't touch with a bargepole. If he got Baxter off…

He would get him off, but Raff also knew a portion of Philip's fee would end up as a cheque to the pensioners Baxter had ripped off. Not all of it—Philip was careful, not stupid with his charity—but the town might end up being grateful. Baxter would think he was great as well.

It was only Raff who'd feel ill, and maybe that was part of ancient history as well. If Philip hadn't been there that night…

How unfair was that?

'Tell us about your wedding dress,' he said, and Abby shot him a look that was both suspicious and angry.

'You want to know—why?'

'Sarah would like to know.'

'I'm going to the wedding,' Sarah said and pointed to the invitation stuck to the fridge. 'You should come, too. Did you get an invitation? Where did you put it? Raff's coming, too, isn't he, Abby?'

'I'm on duty that day,' Raff told her before Abby was forced to answer. 'We talked about it, remember? Mrs Henderson's taking you.'

'It'd be more fun if you were there.'

No, it wouldn't, Raff thought, but he didn't say so. He glanced at his watch. 'I reckon they'll be cooked, Sares.'

'Ooh,' Sarah said, happily distracted. 'My honey jumbles. I could make you some more for your wedding present, Abby. Does Philip like honey jumbles?'

'Sure he does,' Abby said. 'Who wouldn't?'

Honey jumbles. A big cosy kitchen like this. Dogs.

Would Philip like honey jumbles?

Maybe not.

Abby ate four honey jumbles and Sarah beamed the whole time, and how could a girl worry about how tight her wedding dress was going to be in the face of that beam?

Sarah wasn't the only one happy. This morning Kleppy had

been due for the needle. Tonight he was lying under her chair licking the last of Sarah's honey jumbles from his chops.

And Sarah's beam, and Kleppy's satisfaction, and Raff's thoughtful, watchful gaze made her feel…made her feel…

Like she needed to leave before things got out of hand.

She needed to go home to Philip. To tell him she had a dog.

'What's wrong?' Raff asked and he sounded as if he cared. That scared her all by itself. She pushed her chair back so fast she scared Kleppy, which meant she had her dog in her arms and she was at the door before she meant to be.

She hadn't meant to look like she was rushing.

She was rushing.

'Will you take some jumbles in a bag?' Sarah asked and she managed to calm down a little and smile and agree. So Sarah bagged her some jumbles, but she was holding Kleppy, she didn't have a hand free, which meant Raff carried her jumbles down to the car while she carried her dog.

Kleppy was warm and fuzzy. His heart was beating against hers. He was a comfort, she thought, and even as she thought it he stretched up and licked her, throat to chin.

She giggled and Raff, who'd gone before and was stowing her jumbles onto the back seat, turned and smiled in the moonlight.

'Dogs are great.'

'They are,' she said and felt happy.

'Philip will be okay with him?'

Why must he always butt into what wasn't his business? Why must he always spoil the moment?

'He will.'

'So you'll tell him tonight.'

'Of course.'

'I wish you luck.'

'I won't need it.'

'No?'

'Butt out, Finn.'

'You're always saying that,' he said. 'But it's not in my power to butt out. It's my job to intervene in domestic crises. Stopping them before they start is a life skill.'

'You seriously think Philip and I would fight over a dog?'

'I'm thinking you might fight for a dog,' he said softly. 'The old Abby's still there somewhere. She'll fight for this dog to the death.'

'And how melodramatic is that?'

'Melodramatic,' he agreed. 'Call the police emergency number if you need me.'

'Why would I possibly need you?'

'Just offering.' He was holding the passenger door wide so she could pop Kleppy in.

'You know Philip wouldn't…'

'Yeah, I know Philip wouldn't.' He took Kleppy from her and laid him on the passenger seat. 'You're giving him honey jumbles and Kleppy. Why wouldn't the man be delighted?'

'I don't know when I hate it most—when you're being offensive or you're being sarcastic.'

'Maybe they're the same thing.'

'Maybe they are. I wish you wouldn't.'

'No, you don't,' he said softly, 'It helps you keep as far away from me as you want. Isn't that right, Abby?'

'Raff…'

'It's okay, I understand,' he said. 'How could I fail to understand? What you're doing is entirely reasonable. I only wish your second choice wasn't Philip.'

'He's not my second choice. He's my first.'

'That's right,' he said, sounding suddenly thoughtful. 'I forgot. You went out with Philip when you were seventeen. For two whole months and then you dumped him. Don't those reasons hold true now?'

'I can't believe you're asking me…'

'I'm a cop. I ask the hard questions.'

'I don't have to answer.'

'Meaning you can't.'

'Meaning I don't need to. Why are you asking this now?'

'I've hardly had a chance until now. You back off every time you see me.'

'And you know why.'

'I do,' he said harshly and she winced and thought she shouldn't have said it. It was too long ago. The whole thing… It was a nightmare to be put behind them.

'Yes, Philip and I broke up when I was seventeen,' she managed. 'But people change.'

'I guess we do.' He paused and then said, almost conversationally, 'You know, once upon a time we had fun. We even decided we loved each other.'

They had. Girlfriend and boyfriend. Inseparable. Raff had shared her first kiss. It had felt… It had felt…

No. 'We were kids,' she managed. 'We were dumb in all sorts of ways.'

He was too close, she decided. It was too dark. She should be back in her nice safe house waiting for Philip to come home. She shouldn't be remembering being kissed by her first boyfriend.

'I loved kissing you,' he said and it wasn't just her remembering.

'It didn't mean…'

'Maybe it did. There's this thing,' he said.

'What thing?' But she shouldn't have asked because, the moment she had, she knew what he was talking about. Or maybe she'd known all along.

This thing? This frisson, an electric current, an indefinable thing that was tugging her closer…

No. She had to go home. 'Raff…'

'You really want to be Mrs Philip Dexter? What a waste.'

'Leave it!'

'Choose someone else, Abby. Marrying him? You're burying yourself.'

'I am not.'

'Does he make you sizzle?'

'I don't…'

'Does he? You know, I can't imagine it. Good old Philip,

knocking your socks off. Are you racing home now to have hot sex?'

'I don't believe I'm hearing this.'

'You see, it's such a waste,' he said, and suddenly he was even closer, big and bad and dangerous.

Big, bad and dangerous? Certainly dangerous. His hand came up and cupped her chin, forcing her to look up at him, and her sense of danger deepened. But she couldn't pull away.

'I wouldn't mind if it wasn't Philip,' he told her and she wondered if he knew the effect he was having on her. She wondered if he could sense how her body was reacting. 'I've known since Ben died that nothing could bring back what was between you and me. But there are men out there who could bring you alive again. Men who'd like Kleppy.'

'Philip will like Kleppy.'

'Liar.'

He was gazing down into her eyes, holding her to truth.

She should break away. She *could* break away, she thought wildly. He was only holding her chin—nothing more. She could step back, get into the car and drive home.

To Philip.

She could. But he was gazing down into her eyes and he was still asking questions.

'So tell me he makes you sizzle.'

'I...'

'He doesn't, does he?' Raff said in grim satisfaction. 'But there are guys out there who could—who could find out what you're capable of—what's beneath your prissy lawyer uniform. Because you're still there, somewhere. The Abby I...'

He paused. There was a moment's loaded silence when the whole world stilled. *The Abby I...*

She should push away. She should...

She couldn't.

She tilted her face, just a little.

The moment stretched on. The darkness stretched on.

And then he kissed her. As inevitably as time itself, he kissed her.

She couldn't move. She didn't move. She froze. And then…

Heat. Fire. The contact, lips against lips, was a tiny point but that point sizzled, caught, burned and her whole body started heating. Her face was tilted to his but he had no need to hold her. It was as if she was melting against him—into him.

Raff…

He broke away, just a little, and his eyes blazed in the moonlight. 'Abby,' he said and it was a rough, angry whisper. 'Abby.'

'I…'

'Does he do this?' he demanded. He snagged her arms and held them behind her but this was no forceful hold. It was as if her arms might get in the way, could interfere, and nothing must. Nothing could.

She was paralysed, she was burning, but she couldn't escape. She didn't want to escape. What was between them… It sizzled. Tugged as if searching for oxygen.

He was watching her in the moonlight, his eyes questioning. She wouldn't answer. She couldn't.

She was being held by Raff. A man she'd once loved.

She found herself lifting herself, tiptoe.

So her mouth could meet his again.

This morning she'd fantasised about Raff Finn. Sex on legs. But this…

If she'd expected anything it was a kiss of anger, a kiss of sexual tension, passion, nothing more. And maybe it had started like that. But it was changing.

His kiss was tender, aching, even loving. It was as unexpected as ice within a fire, heating, cooling, sizzling all at once. She'd never felt anything like this—she'd never known sensations like this could exist.

Raff.

He'd released her hands and they were free to do as she willed. Her will was that her hands were behind *his* back, drawing him closer, for how could she not want him close?

Sense had flown. Thoughts had flown. There was only this man. There was only this need.

There was only now.

Raff.

Did she say his name?

Maybe she did, or maybe it was just a sigh, deep in her throat, a sound of pure sensual pleasure. Of taking something she'd never dreamed she could have. Of sinking into the forbidden, of the longed for, of a memory she'd have to put away quite soon but not yet, please, not yet.

Oh, but his mouth… Clever and warm and beguiling, it was coaxing her to places she had no business going, but she wanted, oh, she wanted to be there. She was helpless, melting into him, degree by achingly wonderful degree.

He was irresistible.

She was…appalled.

Somehow, she had to break this. Her head was screaming at her, neon danger signs flashing through her sensual need. No!

'No!' It came out a muffled whisper. If he didn't hear…if he ignored it, how could she say it again?

Did she want him to hear it?

But he did, he had, and the wrench as he put her away from him was indescribable. He let her go. He stepped back from her and his eyes in the moonlight were almost as dazed as hers.

But then his face hardened, tightened, and she knew he was moving on.

As she must.

Her mother's voice… *Keep away from the Finn boy. He's trouble.*

He surely was. She was kissing him nine days before her wedding. She was risking all—for the Finn boy?

'I…'

'Just go, Abby,' he said and she didn't recognise his voice. It was harsh and raw and she could even imagine there was pain. 'Get out of here. You know you don't want this.'

'Of course I don't.'

'Then take your dog and go. I'll see you in court.'

Of course she would. She'd see him and he'd be back to being the local cop and she'd be a lawyer sitting beside her fiancé, trying to pretend tonight had never happened.

But it had happened. The feel of his mouth on hers was with her still.

She caught herself, gasped and thumped down into the driver's seat before she could change her mind.

'That was ridiculous,' she managed. 'How...how dare you...?'

'You wanted it as much as I did.'

'Then we're both stupid.'

'We are,' he said gravely. 'We were. But heaven help us, Abby, if we're stupid still.'

CHAPTER FIVE

ABBY drove home in a daze. She felt ill. The feel of Raff's mouth on hers wouldn't go—it felt as if her lips were surely bruised and yet she knew they couldn't be.

There had been tenderness in his kiss. It hadn't been one-sided. He hadn't been brutal.

It had been a kiss of…

No. Don't even think about it.

Kleppy put out his paw in a gesture she was starting to know. Giving comfort as well as taking it. The feel of him beside her was absurdly comforting.

Almost as if he was a little part of Raff…

And there was a dopey thing to think. The whole night had been dopey, she thought. Stupid, stupid, stupid. Imagine if she ever thought there could be anything between herself and Raff. Imagine the heartbreak.

Her heart clenched down. No! Just because the man was a load of semi-controlled testosterone… Just because he had the ability to push her buttons…

She turned into her street and Philip's car was out the front. Her heart sank.

Philip, she told herself. Not a load of semi-controlled testosterone. A good, kind man who'd keep her happy—who'd keep her safe.

I might get tired of safe, she whispered to herself and then she let herself open her mind to the rush of memory that was

Ben and she felt the concept of safe, the need for safe, close around her again. Safe was the only way.

'Hi,' she said, climbing from the car. 'The buck's night finished early, then?'

'Hardly a buck's night.' He took her hands and kissed her and she had to stop herself from thinking *dry as dust.* 'Just my dad and uncles and cousins.'

'Why aren't you having a buck's night?'

'Tonight was enough,' Philip said contentedly. 'I'm busy right up to the honeymoon. Where have you…'

But then he paused. Inside the car, Kleppy had stirred and yawned and whimpered a little.

'What's that?'

Deep breath. 'It's Kleppy.'

'Kleppy?'

'He's my dog,' she said and she had a really good shot at not sounding defensive. Maybe she even succeeded. 'You know Raff gave me a dog this morning and asked me to take him to be put down? I couldn't. He's Isaac Abrahams' dog, he needs a new home and I've decided to keep him. Sarah's been looking after him for me.'

There was no need to mention Raff again. 'So we have a dog,' she said and she surprised herself by sounding cheerful. 'Philip, meet Kleppy. Kleppy, meet Philip. I just know you two are going to be best of friends.'

He didn't like it, but she wouldn't budge; she didn't budge and finally he conceded.

'It'll have to sleep outside.'

'*He,* not *it.*'

'He'll have to sleep outside,' he conceded—no mean concession.

'Okay,' she said with her fingers crossed behind her back. He could sleep outside for a little, she thought, until Philip got used to the idea and then she could sort of sneak him in. And for the next nine nights he could sleep inside at her place.

'And what about our honeymoon?'

'I'll get Mrs Sanderson to feed and walk him.'

'She'll charge.'

'We can afford it.'

'I don't want Eileen Sanderson snooping in our backyard.'

'I'll figure something else out, then. But you'll love him.'

'If you want a dog, then why don't we get a pure-bred?' he asked, checking Kleppy out with suspicion.

'I like Kleppy.'

'And Finn dumped him on you.'

'It was my decision to keep him.'

'You're too soft-hearted.'

'I can't do a thing about that,' she admitted, knowing the hurdle had been leaped and she was over the other side. 'You want to come in for coffee and get acquainted with our new pet?'

'I have work to do. I'm not confident about tomorrow.'

He would be confident, Abby knew, but he'd still go over his notes until he knew them backwards. And once again she wondered—why had he come back to Banksia Bay? He was smart, he was ambitious, he could have made serious money in the city.

'I came back for you,' he'd told her, over and over, but she knew it was more than that. He spent time with her parents. He worked at the yacht club where Ben had once sailed. Every time a challenge occurred that might draw him to the city, he looked at it with regret but he still turned back to Banksia Bay.

She kissed him goodnight and carried Kleppy inside, thinking every time she laid down an ultimatum Philip caved in.

This dog or no wedding?

This dog.

'He loves me,' she told Kleppy, sitting down on the hearth rug and allowing her scruffy dog to settle contentedly on her knee. 'He'll take you because he loves me.'

But she'd seen Philip's ruthless behaviour in court. He could be ruthless. He'd never liked dogs.

Why didn't he just say no?

'I'm so lucky he didn't,' she whispered and she hugged

Kleppy a bit tighter and then gazed towards the spare room door. Her wedding dress lay behind.

She was lucky?

Of course she was.

She was gone and Raff stayed outside, staring sightlessly into the moonlit night.

Abby Callahan.

Right now there was nothing in the world he wanted but Abby Callahan.

Oh, but there was. Inside, Sarah would be snuggling into bed, surrounded by dogs and cats, dreaming of the day she'd just had—her animals, her honey jumbles. Her big brother.

He loved Sarah.

He also loved this place. He loved this town. But love or not, he'd leave if he could. To stay in this place with so many memories…

To stay in this place and watch Abby married…

But leaving wasn't an option. He'd stay and he wouldn't touch her again. Tonight had been an aberration, as stupid as it was potentially harmful. He didn't want to upset Abby. It wasn't her fault she was the way she was.

It was his.

He was thirty years old and he felt a hundred.

He hardly needed to see her again before the wedding. His participation in the Baxter trial was almost over. He'd given the prosecutor all the help he could manage, even if it wasn't enough to convict the guy. There might be another couple of times he was called to the stand, but otherwise he could steer well clear.

So… He'd drop Sarah off at the church next Saturday, pick her up afterwards and it'd be done.

Abby Callahan would be married to Philip Dexter.

Abby spent until midnight making Kleppy hers. She bathed him and blowed him dry with her hairdryer. He was never going to be a beautiful dog, but he was incredibly cute—in a shambolic kind of way. He was a very individual dog, she decided.

He tolerated the hairdryer.

He ate a decent dinner, despite his pre-dinner snack of honey jumbles.

He investigated her bedroom as she got ready for bed. And, curiously, he fell in love with her jewellery box.

It was a beautiful cedar box with inlaid Huon pine. Philip's grandfather had made it for her when she and Philip had announced their engagement. She loved its craftsmanship and she also loved the wood's faint and beautiful perfume, stronger whenever she opened it.

She also loved Philip's grandpa, she thought, as she removed Kleppy's paw from where it had been resting proprietorially on the box. His woodwork was his passion. He'd made these beautiful boxes for half the town. 'It'll last for hundreds of years after I'm gone, girl,' he'd told her and she suspected it would.

Philip's grandpa was part of this town. Philip's family. Her future.

More people's happiness than hers was tied up in next week's wedding. That should make her feel happy, but right now it was making her feel claustrophobic. Which was dumb.

'Do you like the box or the jewels?' she asked Kleppy, deliberately shifting her thoughts. She opened the lid so he could see he couldn't make millions with a jewel heist.

Kleppy nosed the trinkets with disinterest, but looked longingly at the box. He sniffed it again and she thought it was its faint scent he liked.

'No!' she said and put it further back on the chest.

Kleppy sighed and went back to his bra. The bra she'd paid for and given to him. Yes, he shouldn't benefit from crime but today was an exception.

He made a great little thief.

He slept on her bed, snuggled against her, and she loved it. He snored. She loved his snore. She didn't even mind that he slept with his bra tucked firmly under his left front paw.

'Whatever makes you happy, Klep,' she told him, 'but that's the last of your loot. You belong to a law-abiding citizen now.'

One who needs to stay right away from the law.

From Raff.

Don't think of Raff. Think of the wedding.

Some hope. She slept, thinking of Raff.

She woke feeling light and happy. For the past few weeks she'd woken with the mammoth feeling that her wedding was bursting in on her from all sides. Her mother was determined to make it perfect.

It was starting to overwhelm her.

But not this morning. She loved that Kleppy woke at dawn and stuck his nose in her face and she woke to dog breath and a tail wagging.

It was lucky Philip wasn't here. He'd have forty fits.

He wouldn't mind being here. Or rather…he'd be happy if she was *there*. As far as Philip was concerned, she was wasting money having her own little house when he already had a wonderful house overlooking the sea.

Her parents had said that, too. When she'd moved back to Banksia Bay after university they'd welcomed her home and even had her bedroom repainted. Pink.

She had a choice. Philip's house or her old bedroom.

But her grandparents had left her a lovely legacy and this little house was her statement of independence. As she let Kleppy outside to inspect her tiny garden she thought how much she was going to miss it.

Philip's house was fabulous. She'd been blown away that he could afford to build it, and it had everything a woman could possibly want.

So get over it.

She left Kleppy to his own devices and went and checked on her wedding dress—just to reassure herself she really was getting married.

She should be excited.

She was excited. It was a gorgeous dress. It was exquisite. It had taken her two years to make.

The pleasure was in making it. Not in wearing it.

This was dumb. She felt a cold spot on her leg and there was Kleppy, wagging his tail, bright-eyed and bushy-tailed. Looking hopefully at the front door.

Looking for adventure?

'I'll take you round the block before I go to work,' she told him. 'And I'll come home at lunch time. I'm sorry, Klep, but you might be bored this morning. I can't help it, though. It's the price you've paid for me bailing you out of death row.

'And I'm going to be in court this morning, too,' she told him as he looked doleful. 'You're a lawyer's dog and I'm a lawyer. I'm a lawyer with a gorgeous, hand-beaded wedding dress and you're a lawyer's dog with a new home. We need to be grateful for what we have. I'm sure we are.'

She was grateful. It was just, as she left for work and Kleppy looked disconsolately after her, she knew how Kleppy felt.

Raff wasn't in court.

Of course he wasn't. He didn't need to be. He was a cop, not a prosecutor, and he had work to do elsewhere. He'd given his evidence yesterday. Philip wouldn't call him back but she'd sort of hoped the Crown Prosecutor would.

There were things the Crown Prosecutor could ask…

It wasn't for her to know that or even think that—*she was lawyer for the defence*—and it also wasn't for her to have her heart twist because Raff wasn't here.

She slid into the chair beside Philip and he smiled and kissed her and then said, 'Second thoughts about the dog? He really is unsuitable.'

This was what would happen, she thought. He'd agree and then slowly work on her to come round to his way of thinking.

He wasn't all noble.

'No, and I won't be having any,' she said.

'Where is he now?'

'Safely in my garden.' Four-foot fence. Safe as houses.

'He'll make a mess.'

'I walked him before I left. Walking's good. I'm going to do it every morning from now on. Maybe you can join us.'

'Gym's far better aerobic exercise,' he said. 'You need a fully planned programme to get full cardiac advantage. Walking's...'

She was no longer listening.

Her morning had begun.

It was very, very boring.

The hands on the clock moved at a snail's pace.

How bored would Kleppy be?

How bored was she?

Malcolm, the Crown Prosecutor, should do something about his voice, she thought. It was a voice designed to put a girl to sleep.

Ooh, Wallace looked smug.

Ooh, she was bored...

Lunch time. All rise. Hooray.

And then the door of the court swung open.

All eyes turned. As they would. Every person in the room, with the possible exception of Wallace and Philip, was probably as bored as she was.

And suddenly she wasn't bored at all. For standing in the doorway was...Raff.

Full cop uniform. Grim expression. Gun at his side, cop ready for action. At his side—only lower—was a white fluff ball attached to a pink diamanté lead. And in his arms he was carrying Kleppy.

'I'm sorry, Your Honour,' he said, addressing the judge. 'But I'm engaged in a criminal investigation. Is Abigail Callahan in court?'

Of course she was. Abby rose, her colour starting to rise as well. 'K...Kleppy,' she stammered.

'Could you come with me, please, Miss Callahan?' Raff said.

'She's not going anywhere,' Philip snapped, rising and putting his hand on Abby's shoulder. 'What the...'

'If she won't come willingly, I'm afraid I need to arrest her,' Raff said. 'Accessory after the fact.' He looked down at his feet, to where the white fluff ball pranced on the end of her pink diamanté lead. A lead that led up to Kleppy's jaw. Kleppy had a very tight hold. 'Abigail Callahan, your dog has stolen Mrs Fryer's peke. You need to come now and sort this out or I'll have to arrest you for theft.'

The courtroom was quiet. So quiet you could have heard a pin drop.

Justice Weatherby's face was impassive. Almost impassive.

There was a tiny tic at the side of his mouth.

Raff's face was impassive, too. He stood with Kleppy in his arms, waiting for Abby to respond.

Kleppy looked disgusting. He was coated in thick black dust. His tail was wagging, nineteen to the dozen.

In his mouth he held the end of the pink lead and his jaw was clamped as if he wasn't going to let go any time soon.

On the other end of the lead, the white fluff ball was wagging her tail as well.

'He was locked in my backyard,' Abby said, eyeing the two with dismay.

'My sharp investigative skills inform me that the dog can dig,' Raff said, shaking Kleppy a little so a rain of dirt fell onto the polished wood of the courtroom door. 'Will you come with me, please, ma'am?'

'Just give the dog back to whoever owns it,' Philip snapped, his hand gripping Abby's shoulder tightly now. 'Tie the other one up outside. Abigail's busy.'

'Raff, please…' Abby said.

'Mrs Fryer's hopping mad,' Raff said, unbending a little. 'I've waited until court broke for lunch but I'm waiting no longer. You want to avoid charges, you come and placate her.'

She glanced at Philip. Uh-oh. She glanced at Justice Weatherby. The tic at the corner of his mouth had turned into a grin. Someone was giggling at the back of the court.

Philip's face looked like thunder.

'Sort the dog, Abigail,' he snapped, gathering his notes. 'Just get it out of here and stop it interfering with our lives.'

'Right this way, ma'am,' Raff said amiably. 'The solicitor for the defence will be right back, just as soon as she sorts her stolen property.'

Abby walked out behind Raff, trying to look professional, but she didn't feel professional and when she reached the outside steps and the autumn sun hit her face she felt suddenly a wee bit hysterical. And also…a wee bit free?

As if Raff had sprung her from jail.

Which was a dumb thing to think. Raff had attempted to make her a laughing stock.

'I suppose you think you're funny,' she said and Raff turned and looked at her, and once again she was hit by that wave of pure testosterone. He was in his cop uniform and my, it was sexy. The sun was glinting on his tanned face and his coppery hair. He was wearing short sleeves and his arms… They were twice as thick as Philip's, she thought, and then she thought that was a very inappropriate thing to think. As was the fact that his eyes held the most fabulous twinkle.

Her knees felt wobbly.

What was she doing? She was standing in the sun and lusting after Raff Finn. The man who'd destroyed her life…

She needed to get a grip, and fast.

'You're saying Kleppy dug all the way out of my garden?' she snapped, trying to sound disbelieving. She *was* disbelieving.

'You're implying I might have helped?' Raff said, still with that twinkle. 'You think I might have hiked round there and loaned him a spade?'

'No, I…' Of course not. 'But the fence sits hard on the ground. He'd have had to go deep.'

'He's a very determined dog. I did warn you, Abigail.'

'Why don't you just call me ma'am and be done with it,' she snapped. 'What am I supposed to do now?'

'Apologise.'

'To you?'

He grinned at that and his whole face lit up. She'd hardly seen that grin. Not since… Not since…

No. Avoid that grin at all costs.

'I can't imagine you apologising to me,' he said. 'But you might try Mrs Fryer. I imagine she's apoplectic by now. She rang an hour ago to say her dog had been stolen from outside the draper's. I did think we were looking at dog-napping—she'd definitely pay a ransom—but we have witnesses saying the napper was seen making a getaway. It seems Kleppy decided to go find another bra and found something better.'

She closed her eyes. This was not good, on so many levels.

'You caught him?'

'I didn't have to catch him,' he said, and his smile deepened, a slow, smouldering smile that had the power to heat as much as the sun. 'I found the two of them on your front step.'

'On my…'

'He seems to think of your place as home already. Home of Abby. Home of Kleppy. Or maybe he was just bringing this magnificent gift to you.'

Oh, Kleppy.

She stared at her scruffy, kleptomaniac, mud-covered dog in Raff's arms. He stared back, gazing straight at her, quivering with hope. With happiness. A dog fulfilled.

Why did her eyes suddenly fill?

'Why…why didn't you just take Fluffy back to Mrs Fryer?' she managed, trying not to sniff. *She had a dog.*

'Watch this.' He set Kleppy down and tugged the diamanté lead, trying to dislodge it from Kleppy's teeth.

Kleppy held on as if his life depended on it.

Raff tugged again.

Kleppy growled and gripped and glanced across at Abby— and his appeal was unmistakable. *Come and help. This guy's trying to steal your property.*

Her property.

Raff released him. The little dog turned towards her, his

whole body quivering in delight. She stooped and held out her hand and he dropped the lead into it.

Oh, my…

She was having trouble making herself speak. She was having trouble making herself think. This disreputable mutt had laid claim to her.

She should be horrified.

She loved it.

'You could have just taken Fluffy off the other end of the lead,' she managed.

'Hey, your dog growled at me,' Raff said. 'You heard him. He could have taken my hand off.'

'He was wagging his tail at the same time.'

'I'm not one to take chances,' Raff said. 'I might be armed but I'm not a fast draw. Too big a risk.'

She looked up at him, big and brawny and absurdly incongruous. Cop with gun. He'd shoot to kill?

'You don't have capsicum spray?' she managed.

'Lady, you think this vicious mutt could be subdued by capsicum spray?'

She ran her fingers down the vicious mutt's spine. He arched and preened and waggled his tail in pleasure.

The fluff ball moved in for a back scratch as well.

She giggled.

'Abigail…' It was Philip, striding down the steps, looking furious.

Philip. Dignity. She scrambled to her feet and the dogs looked devastated at losing her.

'I'm just settling the dogs down,' she managed. 'Before Raff takes them away.'

'Before *we* take them away,' Raff said. He motioned to his patrol car.

'You can cope with this yourself, Finn,' Philip snapped.

'No,' Raff said, humour fading. He lifted Kleppy in one arm and Fluff Ball in the other. 'You cope with getting Wallace off,' he told Philip. 'Abigail copes with the dogs.'

'I need…'

'You're getting as little help as I can manage to get that low life off the hook,' Raff snapped. 'Abigail, come with me.'

She went. Raff was not giving her a choice, and she knew Mrs Fryer would be furious.

Behind her, Philip was furious but right now that seemed the lesser of two evils.

She sat in the front of Raff's patrol car with two dogs on her knee and she tried to stare straight ahead; to think serious thoughts. She still wanted to giggle.

'Kleppy should be in the back,' Raff said gravely. 'A known criminal.'

'You've accused me of being an accessory. Why don't you toss me in the back as well?'

'I like you up front,' he said. 'You do my image good.'

'I need dark glasses,' she said, glowering. 'Carted round town in a police car.'

'You will keep a kleptomaniac dog. It might well push you over to the dark side. Spoil that good-girl reputation. Send you into the shadowy side, like me.'

Her bubble of laughter faded at that. He'd spoken lightly, but there was truth behind his words.

The shadowy side...

Raff's grandfather and then his mother had given the family a bad name. A drunk and then a woman who'd broken society's rules... If Raff's mother had had the strength to defend herself, to ride out community criticism, then maybe it would have been different but she'd been an easy target. The family had been an easy target.

Raff, though... He had defended himself. He'd come back here after the accident, he'd made a home for Sarah, he'd looked on community disdain with indifference.

Did it hurt?

It wasn't anything to do with her, she thought, but, as they pulled up outside Louise Fryer's, she watched the middle-aged matron greet Raff with only the barest degree of civility. It must still hurt.

After the accident… There'd been no trial.

She remembered the investigators talking to her parents. There'd been insufficient evidence to charge him.

'Is Raff denying it?' That had been Abby, whispering from the background. She barely remembered those appalling days after the crash but she did remember that. She did remember asking. 'What does Raff say?'

'He can't remember a thing,' the investigator told her. 'His blood alcohol's come back zero and frankly that's a surprise. He was just a stupid kid doing stupid things.'

'Our Ben wasn't stupid,' her mother said hotly.

'Led astray, more like,' the investigator said and the fair part of Abby, the reasonable part, thought no, Ben hadn't been wearing his seat belt. It wasn't all Raff's fault.

He'd been stupid. He had been on the wrong side of the dirt road and he'd been speeding.

He'd killed Ben and injured his sister.

Maybe that was enough punishment for anyone. The authorities seemed to think so. Even though her parents wanted him thrown in jail, it had simply been left as an accident.

Raff had come back as the town cop, he'd cared for his sister and he'd worked hard to rid himself of that bad boy reputation. For the most part he now had community respect, but there were those—her parents' friends…people with long memories… He was still condemned.

Louise Fryer, coming out now with her mouth pursed into a look of dislike, was one of the more vocal of the condemners.

'Haven't you found her yet?' Her voice was an accusation. 'I've had five phone calls. People have seen her. Don't you know how valuable she is?'

Abby was trying to untangle leads to get out of the car.

'You don't care,' Mrs Fryer said. 'We need a decent police presence in this… Oh…'

For, finally, Abby was out. She set Fluff Ball on the ground. Fluff Ball headed over to Mrs Fryer.

But… Uh-oh. Kleppy was out of the car and after his prize. He grabbed the lead and Fluff Ball stopped in her tracks.

Fluff Ball looked at Mrs Fryer, then looked at Kleppy. She wagged her pompom and proceeded to check out Kleppy's rear.

'She'll catch something… Get it away…' Louise was practically screeching.

Abby sighed. She picked up both dogs and tucked them firmly under her arms. 'Thank you, Kleppy, but no,' she said severely. She took the lead from Kleppy and handed over Fluff Ball.

And finally Mrs Fryer realised who she was. 'Abigail!'

'Hi, Mrs Fryer.'

'What are you doing here?'

'My dog stole your dog.'

'Your dog?' Louise's eyes were almost popping out of her head. 'That's never your dog.'

'He is. His name's Kleppy. He's lovely but I've only had him for a day so he's not exactly well trained. But he will be.' Just as soon as she installed fences down to bedrock.

'Has this man foisted him onto you?' Her glare at Raff was poisonous.

'No.' Not exactly. Or actually…yes. But that was what the woman was expecting her to say, she thought. Raff Finn— town's bad boy. One of *those* Finns.

Capable of anything.

Which was what she thought, too, she reminded herself, so why was she standing here figuring out how to defend him?

'He didn't foist…' she started.

'Yes, I did,' Raff said before she could get any further. 'Have you forgotten already? I definitely foisted. And that's exactly what you'd expect of someone like me, isn't it, Mrs Fryer? And here I am, messing up your front garden. But it's okay. Your dog's been restored. Justice has been done so I can step out of your life again. If you'll excuse me… Abby, when Mrs Fryer's given you a nice cup of tea so you can both recover from your

Very Nasty Experience, could you walk back to court yourself, do you think?'

I…' She stared at him, speechless. He gave her his very blandest smile.

'I bet Louise wants to hear all about the wedding preparations. She'll be invited, though, won't she?'

'Yes,' Louise said, a bit confused but mostly belligerent. Her dislike for Raff was unmistakable. 'Of course I am. I'm a friend of dear Philip's mother.'

'There you are; you're practically family.' Raff's gaze met hers and there was laughter behind his eyes—pure trouble. 'All it takes for you to be friends for life is for your two dogs to bond, which they're doing already. Me, I have other stuff to do. Murderers and rapists to chase.'

'Or the police station lawn to mow,' Abby snapped and then wished she hadn't.

'I was just saying that to Philip's mother the other night,' Louise said. 'Old Sergeant Troy used to keep the Station really nice.'

'Yeah, but he wasn't a Finn,' Raff said. 'The place has gone to hell in a handbasket since I arrived. Did you think of the lawn yourself, Abigail, or did Philip mention it? A tidy man, our Philip. But enough. Murderers, rapists—and lawn!' He sighed. 'A policeman's lot is indeed a tough one. See you ladies later. Have a nice cup of tea.'

He turned and walked away. Louise put her hand on Abby's arm, holding her back.

The toad. Raff Finn knew she wouldn't be able to get away from here for an hour.

'Make sure you plant some petunias when you're finished,' Abby called after him. 'It'd be a pity if we saw our police force bored.'

'Petunias it is,' he said and gave her an airy wave. 'Consider them planted. In between thefts. How long till the next snatch and grab?' He shook his head. 'Keep off the streets, Abigail, and keep a tight hold on that felon of yours. Next time, I might have to put you up for a community corrections order. The pair of you might find yourself planting my petunias for me.'

CHAPTER SIX

ABBY didn't go back to court. Philip phoned to find out where she was and she decided she had a headache. She did have a headache. Her headache was wagging his tail and watching as she dog-proofed her fence.

According to the Internet, to stop foxes digging into a poultry pen you had to run wire netting underground from the fence, but flattening outward and forward, surfacing about eighteen inches from the fence. The fox would then find itself digging into a U-shaped wire cavity.

That meant a lot of digging. Would it work when Kleppy The Fox was sitting there watching?

'Don't even think about it,' she told him. 'Philip's being very good. We can't expect his patience to last for ever.'

Philip.

She was expecting him to explode. He didn't.

He arrived to see how she was just after she'd finished cleaning up after fence digging. They were supposed to be going out to dinner. Two of Philip's most affluent clients had invited them out to Banksia Bay's most prestigious restaurant as a pre-wedding celebration.

When Abby thought of it her headache was suddenly real—and, surprisingly, she didn't need to explain it to Philip.

'You look dreadful,' he said, hugging her with real sympathy. 'White as a sheet. You should be in bed.'

'I…yes.' Bed sounded a good idea.

'Where's the mutt?'

'Outside.' Actually, on her bed, hoping she'd join him.

'You can't keep him,' Philip said seriously. 'He's trouble.'

'This morning wasn't his fault.'

'You don't need to tell me that,' Philip said darkly. 'The dog might be trouble but Finn's worse. It's my belief he set the whole thing up. Look, Abby, the best thing would just be for you to take the dog back to the Animal Shelter.'

'No.'

He sighed but he held his temper.

'We'll talk about it when you're feeling better. I'm sorry you can't make tonight.'

'Will you cancel?'

'No,' he said, surprised. 'They'll understand.'

Of course they would. They'd hardly notice her absence, she thought bitterly. They'd talk about their property portfolios all night. Make some more money.

'What will you eat?' he asked, solicitous, and she thought she wouldn't have to eat five courses and five different wines. Headaches had their uses.

'I'll make eggs on toast if I get hungry.'

'Well, keep up your strength. You have a big week ahead of you.'

He kissed her and he was off, happily going to a wedding celebration without her.

The moment the door shut behind him, her headache disappeared. Just like that.

Why was she marrying him?

Uh-oh.

The question had been hovering for months. Niggling. Shoved away with disbelief that she could think it. But, the closer the wedding grew, the bigger the question grew. Now it was the elephant in the room. Or the Tyrannosaurus Rex. What was the world's biggest dinosaur?

Whatever. The question was getting very large indeed. And very insistent.

Philip was heading to a dinner she'd been dreading. He was anticipating it with pleasure.

Worse. Philip's kiss meant absolutely nothing. Last night… Raff's kiss had shown her how little Philip's kisses did mean.

And worse still? She'd almost been wanting him to yell at her about Kleppy.

How had she got into this mess?

It had just…happened. The car crash. Philip, always here, supporting her parents, supporting her. Interested in everything she was doing. Throwing himself, heart and soul, into this town. Throwing himself, heart and soul, into her life.

She couldn't even remember when she'd first realised he intended to marry her. It was just sort of assumed.

She did remember the night he'd formally asked. He'd proposed at the Banksia Bay Private Golf Club, overlooking the bay. The setting had been perfect. A full moon. Moonbeams glinting on the sea. The terrace, a balmy night, stars. A dessert to die for—chocolate ganache in the shape of a heart, surrounded by strawberries and tiny meringues. A beautifully drawn line of strawberry coulis, spelling out the words 'Marry Me'.

But there'd been more. Philip had left nothing to chance. The small town orchestra had appeared from nowhere, playing Pachelbel's *Canon*. The staff, not just from the restaurant but from the golf club as well, crowding into the doorways, applauding before she even got to answer.

'I've already asked your parents,' Philip said as he lifted the lid of the crimson velvet box. 'They couldn't be more pleased. We're going to be so happy.'

He lifted the ring she now wore—a diamond so big it made her gasp—and slid it onto her finger before she realised what was happening. Then, just in case she thought he hadn't got it completely right, he'd tugged her to her feet, then dropped to his knees.

'Abigail Callahan, would you do me the honour of becoming my wife?'

She remembered thinking—hysterically, and only for the briefest of moments—what happens if I say no?

But how could she say no?

How could she say no now?

Why would she want to?

Because Rafferty Finn had kissed her?

Because Raff made her feel…

As he'd always made her feel. As if she was on the edge of a precipice and any minute she'd topple.

The night Ben died she'd toppled. Philip had held her up. To tell him now that she couldn't marry him…

What was she thinking? He was a good, kind man and next Saturday she'd marry him and right now she was going to sit in front of the television and stitch a last row of lace onto the hem of her wedding gown. The gown should be finished but her mother and Philip's mother had looked at it and decreed one more row.

'To make everything perfect.'

Fine. Lace. Perfect. She could do this.

She let Kleppy out of the bedroom. He seemed a bit subdued. She gave him a doggy chew and he snuggled onto the couch beside her.

She'd washed him again. He was clean. Or clean enough. So what if the occasional dog hair got on her dress? It didn't have to be that perfect. Life didn't have to be that perfect.

Marriage to Philip would be okay.

The doorbell rang. Kleppy was off the couch, turning wild circles, barking his head off at the door.

He hadn't stirred from his spot on her bed when Philip had rung the bell. Different bell technique?

She should tuck Kleppy back in her bedroom. This'd be her mother. Or Philip's mother. Philip would have reported the headache, gathered the troops. It was a wonder the chicken soup hadn't arrived before this.

Her mother would be horrified at the sight of Kleppy. She'd just have to get used to him, she decided. They'd all have to get used to him. The chicken soup brigade.

But it wasn't the chicken soup brigade.

She opened the door. Sarah was standing on her doorstep holding a gift, and Raff was right behind her.

See, that was just the problem. She had no idea why her heart did this weird leap at the sight of him. It didn't make sense. She should feel anger when she saw him. Betrayal and distress. She'd felt it for ten years but now… Somehow distress was harder to maintain, and there was also this extra layer. Of… hope?

She really didn't want to spend the rest of her life running into this man. Maybe she and Philip could move.

Maybe Raff should move. Why had he come back to Banksia Bay in the first place?

But Sarah was beaming a greeting—Raff's sister—Abby's friend—and Abby thought there were so many complexities in this equation she couldn't get her head around them. Raff was caught as well as she was, held by ties of family and love and commitment.

His teenage folly had killed his best mate. He was trapped in this judgemental town, looking after the sister he loved.

For ten years she'd felt betrayed by this man but she looked at him now and thought he'd been to hell and back. There were different forms of life sentence.

And he'd lost…her?

He'd never had her, she thought fiercely. She'd broken up with him before the crash. If she even started thinking of him that way again…

The problem was, she was thinking. But the nightmare if she kept thinking…

Her parents…Philip… The way she felt herself, the aching void where Ben had been…

She was dealing with it. She had been dealing with it. If only he hadn't kissed her…

'You're home,' Sarah said. She was holding a silver box tied with an enormous red ribbon. 'You took ages to answer. Raff said you probably weren't home. He said you'd be out gall... gall...'

'Gallivanting?'

'It's what I said but I guess that's the wrong word,' Raff said. 'You wouldn't gallivant with Philip.'

She ignored him. She ignored that heart-stopping, dare-you twinkle. 'Hi, Sarah. It's lovely to see you. What do you have there?'

'We're delivering your present,' Sarah said. 'But Raff said you'd be out with Philip. We were going to leave it on the doorstep and go. But I heard Kleppy. Why aren't you out with Philip?'

'I had a headache.'

'Very wise,' Raff said, the gleam of mischief intensifying in those dark, dangerous eyes. 'Dinner with the Flanagans? I'd have a headache, too.'

'How did you know we were going out with the Flanagans?' She sighed. 'No. Don't tell me. This town.'

'Sorry.' Raff's mischief turned to a chuckle, deep and toe-curlingly sexy. 'And sorry about the intrusion, but Sarah wrapped your gift and decided she needed to deliver it immediately.'

'So can we come in while you open it?' Sarah was halfway in, scooping up a joyful Kleppy on the way. But then she faltered. 'Do you still have a headache?' Sarah knew all about headaches—Abby could see her cringe at the thought.

'Abby said she *had* a headache,' Raff said. 'That's past tense, Sares. I reckon it was cured the minute Philip went to dinner without her.'

'Will you cut it out?'

'Do you still have a headache?' he asked, not perturbed at all by her snap.

'No, but...'

'There you go. Sares, what if I leave you here for half an hour so you can watch the present-opening and play with Kleppy? I'll pick you up at eight. Is that okay with you, Abby?'

It wasn't okay with Sarah.

'No,' she ordered. 'You have to watch her open it. It was your idea. You'll really like it, Abby. Ooh, and I want to help you use it.'

So they both came in. Abby was absurdly aware that she had a police car parked in her driveway. That'd be reported to Philip in about two minutes, she thought. And to her parents. And to everyone else in this claustrophobic little town.

What was wrong with her? She loved this town and she was old enough to ignore gossip. Raff was here helping Sarah deliver a wedding gift. What was wrong with that?

Ten minutes tops and she'd have him out of here.

But the gift took ten minutes to open. Sarah had wrapped it herself. She'd used about twenty layers of paper and about four rolls of tape.

'I should use you to design my police cells,' Raff said, grinning, as Abby ploughed her way through layer after layer after layer. 'This sucker's not getting out any time soon.'

'It's exciting,' Sarah said, wide-eyed with anticipation. 'I wonder what it is?'

Uh-oh. Abby glanced up at Raff at that and saw a shaft of pain. Short-term memory… Sarah would have spent an hour happily wrapping this gift, but an hour was a long time. For her to remember what she'd actually wrapped…

There was no way Raff could leave this town, she conceded. Sarah operated on long-term memory, the things she'd had instilled as a child. A new environment…a new home, new city, new friends… Sarah would be lost.

Raff was as trapped here as she was.

But she wasn't trapped, she told herself sharply, scaring herself with the direction her thoughts were headed. She loved it here. She loved Philip.

She was almost at the end. One last snip and…

Ooooh…

She couldn't stop the sigh of pure pleasure.

This was no small gift. It was a thing she'd loved for ever.

It was Gran Finn's pasta maker.

Colleen Finn had been as Irish as her name suggested. She was one of thirteen children and she'd married a hard drinking bull of a man who'd come to Australia to make a new start with no intention of changing his ways.

As a young bride, Gran had simply got on with it. And she'd cooked. Every recipe she could get her hands on, Irish or otherwise.

Abby was about ten when the pasta maker had come into the house. Bright and shiny and a complete puzzle to them all.

'Greta Riccardo's having a yard sale, getting rid of all her mother's stuff.' Gran was puffed up like a peahen in her indignation. 'All Maria's recipes—books and books—and here's Greta saying she never liked Italian food. That's like me saying I don't like potatoes. How could I let the pasta maker go to someone who doesn't love it? In honour of my friend Maria, we'll learn to be Italian.'

It was in the middle of the school holidays and the kids, en masse, were enchanted. They'd watched and helped, and within weeks they'd been making decent pasta. Abby remembered holding sheets of dough, stretching it out, competing to see who could make the longest spaghetti.

Pasta thus became a staple in the Finn house and it was only as she grew older she realised how cheap it must have been. With her own eggs and her home grown tomatoes, Gran had a new basic food. But now...

'Don't you use this any more?' she ventured, stunned they could give away this part of themselves, and Raff smiled, though his smile was a little wary.

And, with the wariness, Abby got it.

She remembered Sarah as a teenager, stretching dough, kneading it, easing it through the machine with care so it wouldn't rip, making angels' hair, every kind of the most delicate pasta varieties.

She thought of Sarah now, with fumbling fingers, knowing what she'd been able to do, knowing what she'd lost.

'We don't use it any more,' Sarah said. 'But we don't want

to throw it away. So Raff said why don't we give it to you and I can come round and remind you how to do it.'

'Will you and I make some now?' she asked Sarah before she could stop herself. 'Can you remember how to make it?'

'I think so,' Sarah said and looked doubtfully at her big brother. 'Can I, Raff?'

'Maybe we could both give Abby a reminder lesson,' Raff said. 'As part of our wedding present. If your headache's indeed better, Abigail?'

Both? Whoa. No. Uh-uh.

This was really dumb.

The police car would be parked outside for a couple of hours.

'You want me to drive the car round the back?' he asked.

She stared at him and he gazed straight back. Impassive. Reading her mind?

This was up to her. All she had to do was say her headache had come back.

They were all looking at her. Sarah. Kleppy.

Raff.

Go away. You're complicating my life. My wedding dress is right behind that door. My fiancé is just over the far side of town.

Sarah's eyes were wide with hope.

'I guess it'll still get around that my car was round the back for a couple of hours,' Raff said, watching the warring emotions on her face. 'Will Dexter call me out at dawn?'

'Philip,' she said automatically.

'Philip,' he agreed. Neutral.

'He won't mind,' she said.

'I'd mind if I was Philip.'

'Just lucky you're not Philip,' she said and she'd meant to sound snarky but she didn't quite manage it. 'Why don't you go do what you need to do and come back in a couple of hours?'

'But Raff likes making pasta, too,' Sarah said and Abby looked at his face and saw…and saw that he did.

There was a lot of this man to back away from. There was a lot about this man to distrust. But watching him now… It was as if he was hungry, she thought. He was disguising it, with his smart tongue and his teasing and his blatant provocation, but still…

He'd just given away his grandmother's pasta maker. He'd given it to her.

She'd love it. She'd use it for ever. The memories… She and Sarah, Raff and Ben, messing round in Gran's kitchen.

If it wasn't for this man, Ben would still be here.

How long did hate last?

For the last ten years, every time she'd looked at Raff Finn she'd felt ill. Now… She looked at Sarah and at the pasta maker. She thought of Mrs Fryer's vitriol. She thought that Ben had been Raff's best friend. Ben had loved him.

She'd loved him.

She couldn't keep hating. She just…couldn't.

She felt sick and weary and desperately sad. She felt… wasted.

'Hey, Abby really isn't well,' Raff said and maybe he'd read the emotions—maybe it was easy because she was having no luck disguising them from herself, much less from him. 'Maybe we should go, Sares, and let her recover.'

'Do you really have a headache?' Sarah put her hand on her arm, all concern. 'Does it bang behind your eyes? It's really bad when it does that.'

Did Sarah still have headaches? Did Raff cope with them, take care of her, ache for his little sister and all she'd lost?

Maybe she should have invited Raff to her wedding.

Now there was a stupid thing to think. She might be coming out the other side of a decade of bitterness but her parents… they never would. They knew that Raff had killed their son, pure and simple.

Philip would never countenance him at their wedding. Her parents would always hate him.

Any bridges must be her own personal bridges, built of an

understanding that she couldn't keep stoking this flame of bitterness for the rest of her life.

They were watching her. Sarah's hand was still on her arm. Concerned for her headache. Sarah, whose headaches had taken away so much…

'Not a headache,' she whispered and then more strongly, 'it's not a headache. It's just… I'm overwhelmed. I loved making pasta with you guys when I was a kid. I can't believe you're giving this to me. It's the most wonderful gift—a truly generous gift of the heart. It's made me feel all choked up.'

And then, as Sarah was still looking unsure, she took her hands and tugged her close and kissed her. 'Thank you,' she whispered.

'Raff, too,' Sarah said.

Raff, too. He was watching with eyes that were impassive. Giving nothing away.

He'd given her his grandmother's pasta maker.

He'd killed her brother.

No. An accident had killed Ben. A moment of stupidity that he'd have to pay for forever.

She took a deep breath, released Sarah, took Raff's hands in hers and kissed him, too. Lightly. As she'd kissed Sarah.

On the cheek and nothing more.

She went to release him but he didn't release her. His hands held for just a fraction of a second too long. A fraction of a second that said he was as confused as she was.

A fraction of a second that said there could never be idle friendship between them.

No longer enemies? But what?

Not friends. Not when he looked at her like… Like he was seeing all the regret in the world.

She had to do something. They were all looking at her—Raff, Sarah and Kleppy. Wondering why her eyes were brimming—why she was standing like a dummy wishing the last ten years could disappear and she could be seventeen again and Raff could be gorgeous and young and free and…

And she needn't think anything of the kind. In eight days she was marrying Philip. Her direction was set.

Eight days was all very well, but what about now?

Now she closed her eyes for a fraction of a second, gave herself that tiny respite to haul herself together—and then she put on her very brightest smile.

'Let's make pasta,' she said, and they did.

CHAPTER SEVEN

HE SHOULDN'T have given the pasta maker away if it made him feel like this.

This was a bad idea and it was getting worse.

He was sitting at Abby's kitchen table watching Sarah hold one end of the pasta dough as Abby fed it through the machine. Watching it stretch. Watching Sarah hold her breath, gasp with pleasure, smile.

Watching Abby smile back.

He could help—Sarah kept offering him a turn—but he excused himself on the grounds that all Abby's aprons were frilly and there was no way Banksia Bay's cop could be caught in a rose-covered pinny.

But in reality he simply wanted to watch.

He'd forgotten how good it was to watch Abby Callahan.

Had she forgotten how to be Abby Callahan?

For years now, he'd never seen her with a hair out of place. Now, though, she was wearing faded jeans, an old sweatshirt smudged with flour, bare feet.

He remembered her in bare feet.

Abby. Seventeen years old. She'd laugh and everyone laughed with her. She could tease a smile out of anyone. She was a laughing, loving girl.

She'd been his girlfriend and he'd loved it. They just seemed to...fit.

But then they'd grown up. Sort of.

One heated weekend. Angry words. The car. The debutante ball. Incredibly important to teenagers.

Abby had started dating Philip. She and Philip had broken up, and then Sarah had started going out with him.

He hadn't liked that, either. Maybe he'd acted like a jerk, making Abby pay. He'd assumed they'd make it up.

But then... The tragedy that turned Abby from a girl who'd dreamed of being a dress designer, who lived for colour and life, into a lawyer who represented the likes of Wallace Baxter.

A lawyer who was about to marry Philip Dexter.

No.

He came close to shouting it, to thumping his fist down on the flour-covered table.

He did no such thing. There was no reason why she shouldn't marry Philip. There was nothing Raff could put his finger on against the guy. Philip was a model citizen.

He didn't like him.

Jealous?

Yeah. But something else. A feeling?

A feeling he'd had at nineteen that had never gone away.

'Why did you and Dexter stop going out?' he asked as the pasta went through a third and final time.

She didn't lift her head but he saw the tiny furrow of concentration, the setting of her lips.

'Abby?'

'Just ease it in a little more, Sarah.'

'Ten years ago. After your debut. Why did you break up?'

'That's none of your business. Now we put this attachment on to cut it into ribbons.'

'I know,' Sarah said, crowing in triumph as she found the right attachment. 'This one.'

'It's just I've always wondered,' Raff said as Sarah tried to get the attachment in. They both let her be. It'd be easier to step in and do it for her—her fingers were fumbling badly—but she was a picture of intense concentration and to step in now...

They both knew not to.

'You know I only went out with Debbie Macallroy to get back at you,' he said.

'So you did. Childhood romances, Raff. We were dumb.'

Really dumb. Where had they all ended up?

'We did have fun before the crash,' he said gently. 'We were such good friends. But then Philip… First you and then Sarah. But you didn't fall in love with him then. You ditched him.'

'I've changed. We both have.'

'People don't change.'

'Of course they do.'

Of course people changed. She had, and so had Philip.

She didn't look up at Raff; she focused on the sheets of pasta, making sure they were dusted so they wouldn't stick in the final cutting process.

She thought back to Philip at nineteen.

He'd been rich, or rich compared to every other kid in Banksia Bay. He had his own car and it was a far cry from the bomb Ben and Raff were doing up. A purple Monaro V8. Cool.

Every girl in Abby's year group had wanted to go out with him. Abby didn't so much—she was trying hard not to think she was still in love with Raff—but she'd needed a partner for her debut, all Raff thought about was his stupid car, and Sarah had bet her she wouldn't be game to ask him.

For a few weeks she'd preened. Her friends were jealous. Philip danced really well and her debut was lovely.

But what followed…the drive-in movies… Sitting in the dark with Philip… Not so cool. Nothing she could put her finger on, though. It was just he wasn't Raff and that was no reason to break up with him.

But finally…

They'd gone for a drive one afternoon, heading up Black Mountain to the lookout. She hadn't wanted to go, she remembered, and when they'd had a tyre blowout she'd been relieved.

She hadn't been so relieved when they realised Philip's spare tyre was flat. Or when he thought she should walk back into town to fetch his father—because he had to look after the car.

'No way am I trudging back to town while you sit here in comfort,' she retorted. 'You're the dummy who didn't check his spare.'

Not so tactful, even for a seventeen-year-old, but she was reaching the point where she wanted to end it.

Philip left her. Bored, she tried out the sound system. His tapes were boring, top ten stuff, nothing she enjoyed.

She flicked through his tape box—a box just like the one that graced her bedside table, beautiful cedar with slots for every cassette. His grandpa really was great.

Boring cassettes. Boring, boring. But, at the back, some unmarked ones. She slid one in and heard the voice of Christabelle Thomas, a girl in the same class as her at school.

'Philip, we shouldn't. My mum'd kill me. Philip...'

Enough. She met Philip and his father as she stomped down the mountain, fuming.

'You were supposed to stay with the car,' Philip told her.

'I didn't like the music,' she snapped, and held up the tape and threw it at him through his father's car window. 'Put the ripped up tape in my letterbox tomorrow or I'm telling Christabelle.'

Why think of that now?

Because of Raff?

She glanced up and he was watching her. Sarah was watching her.

'What's wrong?' Sarah asked, and she came back to the present and realised Sarah had successfully put the cutting tool in place.

'Hey, fantastic, let's cut,' she said, and the moment had passed. The time had passed. The tapes had been an aberration.

Philip had brought the tape round the next morning, cut to shreds.

'Hey, Abby, I need to tell you I'm sorry. Christabelle and I only went out a couple of times, well before you and me. It's not what you think. I only asked to kiss her. And I hadn't realised the tape was on record. I record stuff in the car all the time on the trip between here and Sydney—I try and recall study notes and then see how accurate I've been. I must have forgotten this was still on. I'm so sorry you found it.'

It was okay, she conceded. It was a mistake. Kids did stupid things.

Like driving on the wrong side of the road?

'What's wrong?' Sarah asked again and Raff's eyes were asking the same question.

'Sorry,' she said. 'I just started thinking about all the things I had to do before the wedding.'

'You want us to go home?' Sarah asked, and Abby winced and got a grip.

'No way. I'm hungry. Pasta, here we come. What setting shall we have it on? Do we want angels' hair or tagliatelle?'

'Angels' hair,' Sarah said.

'My favourite,' Raff said. 'It always has been.'

She glanced up and he was looking straight at her. He wasn't smiling.

Raff…

Don't, she told herself but she wasn't quite sure what she was saying *don't* to.

All she knew was that this man meant trouble. He was surely causing trouble now.

They left at nine, which gave her an hour to clean the kitchen and to get her thoughts in order before Philip arrived.

He arrived promptly at ten. Kleppy met him at the door and growled.

He hadn't growled at Raff and Sarah, but then he knew they were friends.

He didn't yet know Philip was a friend.

'If he bites…' Philip said.

'He won't bite. He's being a watchdog.'

'I thought you had a headache,' Philip said, wary and ir-ritated. 'I hear Finn and his sister have been here.'

She sighed. She lived in Banksia Bay. She should be used to this.

'Sarah brought our wedding present. She wanted to demonstrate.'

'Demonstrate what?'

'Her gran's pasta maker. You need to see it, Philip. It's cool.'

'A second-hand pasta maker?'

'It's an heirloom.'

'Pasta makers aren't heirlooms.'

'This one is.' She gestured to the battered silver pasta maker taking pride of place on her bench. 'We'll make pasta once a week for the rest of our lives. When we're finally in our nurs-ing home we'll discuss the virtues of each of our children and decide who most deserves our fantastic antique pasta maker. If our children are unworthy we'll donate it to the State Gallery as a National Treasure.'

He didn't even smile. 'You said you had a headache.'

'I did have a headache.'

'But you let them in.'

'It was Sarah,' she said, losing patience. 'Her gran's pasta maker means a lot to her. She was desperate to see me using it.'

'You weren't well enough to come out to dinner.'

'If it was necessary I would have come,' she snapped. 'It wasn't. It was, however, absolutely necessary for me to show Sarah that her grandmother's pasta maker will be appreciated.'

'And Finn?'

'You mean Raff?'

'Of course I mean Raff. Finn.'

'He brought Sarah here. He watched.'

'I don't see how you can bear that man to be in the house.'

'I can bear a lot for Sarah.'

'Even having a dog foisted onto you.'

Kleppy growled again and Abby felt like growling herself. 'Philip...'

And, just like that, he caved. He put his hands up in mock surrender, tossed his jacket over the back of a kitchen chair and hugged her. Kissed her on the forehead.

'Sorry. Sorry, sorry. I know you had no choice. I know you wouldn't let Finn in unless you had no choice.'

Of course she wouldn't.

'Tell me about tonight,' she said, and he sat and she made him coffee and he told her all about the fantastic business opportunities they'd discussed—projects of mutual benefit that needed careful legal input if they were to get past council.

And all the while... Things were changing.

Some time in the last twenty-four hours the buried question had surfaced in her head and it was getting louder and louder until it was almost a drumbeat.

Why am I marrying this man?

The question was making her feel dizzy.

A week on Saturday she'd be married to Philip.

Uh-oh.

This was Raff's fault, she thought, feeling desperate. Raff asking her...

Why did you and Dexter stop going out?

She'd shoved that memory away ten years ago, not to be thought of again. Remembering it now... How she'd felt...

Underneath the logic, did she still feel like that?

This was like waking from a coma. A million emotions were crowding in. Memories. Stupid childhood snatches. Laughter, trouble, tears, adventure, fun...

Always with Raff.

'Philip, I...'

'You need to go to bed,' he said, immediately contrite. He

rose. 'I'm sorry, I forgot the headache. You should have said. Just because Finn barges his way in, welcome or not... I have a bit more finesse. You sleep well and I'll see you in the morning. Breakfast at the yacht club? You want to come sailing afterwards?'

'Mum's organised the girls' lunch at midday.'

'Of course. So much to plan...'

So much to plan? This wedding had been organised for years.

'Sleep well, sweetheart,' he told her and stooped and kissed her. Dry. Dusty. He reached for his jacket...

And paused. Frowned. Felt the pockets. 'My wallet.'

'Your wallet?'

'It was in my side pocket.'

'Could you have dropped it?'

'It was there when I got out of the car.' He opened the front door and stared out at the path. The front light showed the path smooth and bare. 'I always check I have my phone and my wallet when I get in and out of the car.'

Of course. Caution was Philip's middle name.

'I'm sure I didn't drop it,' he said.

Which left... She swivelled and looked for Kleppy.

Kleppy was at her bedroom door. He had something on the floor in front of him.

A wallet? Too big?

She walked over to see and he wagged his tail and beamed up at her. She was sure it was a beam. It might be the stupidest beam on the planet but it was strangely adorable.

'What have you got?'

It wasn't the wallet. It was her jewellery box, the cedar box Philip's grandfather had given her. Her heart sank. If he'd chewed it...

He hadn't.

How had he got it down from the bedside table?

There wasn't a mark on it. He had his paw resting proprietorially on its lid but when she bent down and took it he quivered all over with that stupid canine beam. *Aren't I fantastic? Look what I found for you!*

'That dog…' Philip said in a voice full of foreboding.

'He doesn't have it,' she said. 'But…'

She looked more closely at Kleppy. Then she looked at her bed.

Kleppy had retrieved the box via the bed. She had a pale green quilt on her bed. The coverlet was now patterned with footprints.

She bent down and looked at Kleppy's paws.

Dirt.

Uh-oh, uh-oh, uh-oh.

She looked out through the glass doors to the garden. To the fence. To where she'd dug in netting all the way along.

Lots of lovely loose soil. A great place to bury something.

Loose dirt was scattered over the grass in half a dozen places. Kleppy, it seemed, had been a little indecisive in his burial location.

'You're kidding me,' Philip said, guessing exactly what had happened.

'Uh-oh.' What else was a girl to say?

'You expect me to dig?'

'No.' She'd had enough. She was waking from a bad dream and this was part of it.

'I'll find it,' she told him. 'I'll give it to you in the morning.'

'Clean.'

'Clean,' she snapped. 'Of course.'

'It's not my fault the stupid…'

'It's not your fault,' she said, cutting him off. It never was. Of all the childish…

No. She was being petulant herself. She needed to get a grip. She needed to find the wallet and then think through what was important here. She needed to decide how she could do the unimaginable.

'Of course it's not your fault,' she said more gently and

she headed outside to start sifting dirt. 'I took Kleppy on. I'm responsible. Go home, Philip, and let me sort the damage my way.'

'I can help…' he started, suddenly unsure, but she shook her head.

'My headache's come back,' she said. 'I can use a bit of quiet digging. And thinking.'

'What do you need to think about?'

'Weddings,' she said. 'And pasta makers. And dogs.'

And other stuff she wasn't even prepared to let into the corners of her mind until Philip was out of the door.

She dug.

She should have thought and dug, but she just dug. Her mind felt as if it had been washed clear, emptied of everything.

What was happening? Everything she'd worked for over the last ten years was suddenly…nothing.

Stupid, stupid, stupid.

This is just pre-wedding nerves, she told herself. But she knew it was more.

She dug.

It was strangely soothing, delving into the soft loam, methodically sifting. She should be wearing gardening gloves. She'd worn gardening gloves this afternoon when she'd laid the netting, but that was when it mattered that she kept her nails nice. That was when she was going to get married.

There was a scary thought. She sat back on her heels and thought, *Did I just think that?*

How could she not get married?

Her dress. Two years in the making. Approximately two thousand beads.

Two hundred and thirty guests.

People were coming from England. People had already come from England.

Her spare room was already filling with gifts.

She'd have to give back the pasta maker.

And that was the thing that made her eyes suddenly fill with tears. It made her realise the impossibility of doing what she was thinking of.

Handing Raff Finn back the pasta maker and saying, *Here, I can't accept it—I'm not getting married.*

Why Raff? Why was his gift so special?

She knew why. She knew…

The impossibility of what she was thinking made her choke. This was stupid. Nostalgia. Childhood memories.

Not all childhood memories. Raff yesterday at the scene of the accident, standing in front of her car, giving orders.

Raff, caring about old Mrs Ford.

Raff…

'We always wish for what we can't have,' she muttered to herself and shoved her hand deep into the loam so hard she hit the wire netting and scraped her knuckles.

She hauled her hand out and an edge of leather came with it.

She stared down at her skinned knuckle and Philip's wallet.

She needed a hug.

'Kleppy,' she called. 'I found it. You want to come lick it clean?'

Fat chance. It was a joke. She should be smiling.

She wasn't smiling.

'Kleppy?'

He'd be back on her bed, she thought. How long till he came when she called?

'Kleppy?' She really did want a hug. She wiped away the dirt and headed inside.

No Kleppy.

How many hiding places were there? Where was he?

Not here.

Not in the house.

The front door was closed. He could hardly have opened it and walked out. He was clever but not…

Memory flooded back. Philip, throwing open the door to stare at the front path. She'd gone to look for Kleppy, then she'd headed straight out to the garden.

Philip leaving. Slamming the door behind him.

The door had been open all the time they'd talked.

Her heart sank. She should have checked. She'd been too caught up with her own stupid crisis, her own stupid pre-wedding jitters.

Kleppy was gone.

CHAPTER EIGHT

ABBY searched block by block, first on foot and then fetching the car and broadening her search area.

How far could one dog get in what—half an hour? More? How long had she sat out in the garden angsting about what she should or shouldn't be doing with her life?

How had one dog made her question herself?

Where was he?

She wanted to wake up the town and make them search, but even her friends... To wake them at midnight and say, *Please, can you help me find a stray dog?* was unthinkable.

They'd think she was nuts.

Sarah wouldn't think she was nuts. Or Raff.

Her friends...

She thought of the kids she'd messed around with when she was a kid. They'd dropped away as she was seen as Philip's girl. Philip's partner. Philip's wife?

Those who remained... She winced, wondering how she'd isolated herself. She'd done it without thinking. How many years had she simply been moving forward with no direction? Or in Philip's direction. So now, who did she call when she was in the kind of trouble Philip disapproved of?

She knew who.

No.

She searched for another hour.

One o'clock.

This was crazy. She couldn't do it by herself.

Do not go near Raff Finn. That man is trouble. It had been a mantra in her head for years but now it had changed. Trouble had taken on a new dimension—a dimension she wasn't brave enough to think about.

She pushed the thought of Raff away and kept searching. Wider and wider circles. A small dog. He'd be safe until morning, she told herself. He had street smarts. He was a stray.

He wasn't a stray. He was Isaac Abrahams' loved dog. He wore his owner's medal of valour on his collar.

He was *her* Kleppy.

She drove on. Round the town. She walked through the deserted mall. She walked out onto the wharves at the harbour.

And then? There was only one place left to search. Isaac's.

Up the mountain in the dark? To Isaac's? She hated that place. She couldn't.

He had to be somewhere. After this time, logic said that was where he'd be.

She couldn't make herself go alone. She just…couldn't.

Don't do it.

Do it.

At two in the morning she phoned the police. The police singular.

Raff's patrol car pulled up outside her front door ten minutes after she called. He had the lights flashing.

He swung out of the car, six feet two inches of lethal cop. Ready for action.

She'd been parked, waiting for him. In the dark. Not wanting to wake the neighbours. His flashing lights lit the street and curtains were being pulled.

'Turn the lights off,' she begged.

'This is Kleppy,' he said seriously. 'I thought about sirens.'

'You want to wake the town?'

'How much do you want to find him?'

'A lot,' she snapped and then caught herself. 'I mean… please.'

'So how did you lose him? You let him out?'

'I…yes.'

He looked at her face and got an answer. 'Dexter let him out.'

'By mistake.'

'I'm sure.'

'By mistake,' she snapped.

'How long ago?'

'Three hours.'

'Three hours? You've only just discovered he's missing?' There was a whole gamut of accusation in his tone. Like what had she and Philip been doing for three hours that they hadn't noticed they'd lost a dog?

'I've been searching,' she said through gritted teeth. 'Can we just… I don't know…'

'Find him?' he suggested, and suddenly his voice was gentle. The switch was nearly her undoing. She was so close to tears.

'Yes. Please.'

'Where have you looked?'

'Everywhere.'

'That just about covers it. You sure he's not under your bed?'

'I'm sure.'

'That's where we find most missing kids,' he said. 'Within two hundred yards of the family refrigerator.'

'You want to look again?'

'I trust you. Is Dexter out hunting?'

Silence. She wasn't going to answer. She didn't need to answer.

'I'm…I'm sorry to call you out,' she ventured.

'This is what I do.'

'Hunt for lost dogs when you should be home with Sarah?'

'Sarah's used to me being out in the night. She has her dogs.'

'Are you on duty?'

'This is a two cop town. When there's an emergency, Keith and I are both on.'

'This is an emergency?'

'Kleppy's definitely an emergency,' he said. 'He's a loved dog with an owner. I was never more relieved than when you said you'd take him on. For all sorts of reasons,' he said enigmatically, but then kept right on. 'You want to ride with me? We'll check out Main Street. Morrisy Drapers is his favourite spot.'

'I've been there. It's all locked up. The bargain bins are inside. No Kleppy.'

'You've what?' he demanded, brow snapping. 'You walked the mall alone?'

'This is Kleppy.'

'At two on a Saturday morning? There's the odd drunk and nothing else in the mall.'

'Yeah, and no Kleppy.'

His mouth tightened but he said nothing, turning the car towards the waterfront. 'He likes the harbour, our Kleppy. Isaac's been presented with a live lobster before now. Isaac had to get Kleppy's nose stitched but he got him home, live and fighting.'

'Oh,' she said and choked on a bubble of laughter that was close to hysteria. 'A lobster?'

'Almost bigger than he was. Cost Isaac a hundred and thirty dollars for the lobster and another three hundred at the vet's. They had a great dinner that night.'

He had his flashing lights on again now. He hit another switch and floodlights lit both sides of the road.

The law on the hunt.

'I've checked the harbour,' she said in a small voice, already knowing the reaction she'd get.

And she did.

'Also by yourself.' His tone was suddenly angry. 'Hell, woman, you know the dropkicks go down there at night.'

'They haven't seen Kleppy.'

'You asked?'

'This is Kleppy.'

'You asked. You approached the low life that crawl round that place at night? Where the hell is Dexter?'

'In bed,' she snapped. She caught herself, fighting back anger in response. 'I know I should have phoned him but he's not…he's not quite reconciled to having a dog.'

'Which is why he left the door open.'

'He did not do it deliberately.'

'You make one stubborn defence lawyer,' he said more mildly and went back to concentrating on the sides of the road.

She fumed. Or she tried to fume. She was too tired and too worried to fume.

'Have you tried up the mountain?' Raff asked and she caught her breath.

The mountain.

Isaac's place.

'N… No.' She swallowed. Time to confess. 'That's why… that's why I called you.'

'You didn't go up there?'

'I haven't. Not since…' She paused. Tried to go on. Couldn't.

Tonight she'd walked a deserted shopping mall. Tonight she'd fronted a group of very drunk youths down at the harbour to ask if they'd seen her dog.

But the place with the most fears was Kleppy's home. Isaac's place.

Up the mountain where Ben had been killed. To go there at night…

The last night she'd been there would stay in her mind for ever. The phone call. The rain, the dark, the smell of spilled gasoline, the sight of…

'It's just a place, Abby,' Raff said gently. 'You want to stay home while I check?'

'I…no.' She had to get over this. Ten years. She was stuck in a time warp, an aching void of loss. 'I'm sorry. You must hate going up there, too.'

'There's lots of things I hate,' he said softly. 'But going up the mountain's not one of them. It's Isaac's home. He was a great old guy.'

He was. She remembered Isaac the night of the accident. Of course he'd heard the crash; he'd been first on the scene. He'd been cradling Ben when she'd got there.

All the more reason to love his dog. All the more reason to face down her hatred of the place.

'You know, you can't block it out for ever,' Raff said. 'Work it through and move on.'

'Like you have.' She heard the anger in her words and flinched.

'Like I try to,' Raff said evenly. 'It always hurts but limbo's not my idea of a great time. You want to spend the rest of your life there?'

'What's that supposed to mean?'

'Meaning you've never come back,' he said. 'You're as damaged as Sarah is in your own way.'

She shook her head. 'No. No, I'm not. I'm fine. Just find my dog, Raff.'

'I'll do my best,' he said gravely. 'You know, taking Kleppy's a great start. Kleppy's forcing chinks in your lawyerish armour and I'm not so sure you can seal them up again. Let's see if we can find him so he can go the whole way.'

Isaac's place was locked and deserted, a ramshackle homestead hidden in bushland. Through the fence, they could see Isaac's garden, beautiful in the moonlight, but they couldn't get in the front gate. The gate was padlocked and a cyclone fence had been erected around the rickety pickets.

'Isaac's daughter's worried about vandalism before she can get the place on the market,' Raff said. 'She sacked the gardener, hired a security firm and put the fence up.' Raff headed off, striding around the boundary, searching the ground with his flashlight as well as through the fence. Abby had to run to catch up with him.

The ground was unsteady. Raff's hand was suddenly holding hers. She should pull away—but she didn't.

'Call him,' Raff said.

She called, her voice ringing out across the bushland, eerie in the dark.

'Keep calling.' Raff's hand held hers, strong and warm and pushing her to keep going.

'We'll call from the other side,' he said. 'If he's down nearer the road…'

Near the road where Ben was killed?

Move on. She did move on, and Raff's hand gave her the strength to do it. How inappropriate was that?

But she called. And she called. And then, unbelievably…

Out through the bush, tearing like his life depended on it, Kleppy came flying. Straight to her.

She gasped and stooped to catch him and the little dog was in her arms, wriggling with joy. She was on her knees in the undergrowth, hugging. Maybe even weeping.

'Hey, Klep,' Raff said, and she could hear his relief. 'Where have you been hiding?'

She hugged him tight and he licked her…then suddenly he wrenched out of her arms, backed off and barked—and tore back into the bush.

Raff made a lunge for him but he was too fast.

He disappeared back into the darkness.

'You could have held his collar,' Raff said, but he didn't sound annoyed. He sounded resigned.

'Oh, my…' She started to run, but Raff put his hand out and stopped her.

'We walk. We don't run. Wombat holes, logs, all sorts of traps for the unwary in the dark.'

'But Kleppy…'

'Won't have gone far,' he said, taking her hand firmly back into his. 'You saw him—he was joyful to see you. This is Isaac's place, Kleppy's territory, but I reckon you're his now. It seems you're his person to replace Isaac. That's a fair responsibility, Abby Callahan. I hope you're up to it.'

'Just find him for me,' she muttered.

Kleppy's person?

She didn't want to think about where that was taking her.

She didn't actually want to think at all.

Kleppy had headed back down the hill. Towards the road. They were now within two hundred yards of where the cars had crashed.

It had rained this week. The undergrowth smelled of wet eucalypt, scents of the night, scents she hated.

She'd never wanted to come back here.

'Move on,' Raff said, holding her hand tightly. 'You can.'

She couldn't.

The thought that it had been Raff, the man holding her hand right now...

Raff...

She could not depend on this man. This man was dangerous; he always had been. He'd been dangerous to Ben. Now suddenly he seemed dangerous in an entirely different way.

But he was the one searching for Kleppy, not Philip.

That would have to be thought about tomorrow. For now... just get through tonight.

'If he's gone back down to the town...'

'Why would he do that? This is Isaac's place. You're here. Everything he knows is here.' And then, before she could respond, his flashlight stopped moving and focused.

Kleppy was fifty yards from the road. Digging? He was nosing his way through the undergrowth, pawing at the damp earth, wagging, wriggling, digging...

'Kleppy...' she called and started towards him.

Kleppy looked up at her—and headed back in the direction he'd come from. Back to Isaac's.

Raff sighed.

'You don't make a very good cop,' he said. 'Letting the suspect go. Sneaking up and then breaking into a run at the last minute.'

'What's he doing?' They were following him again, back

through the undergrowth. Once more, Raff had her hand. She absolutely should let it go.

She didn't.

'I suspect he's one very confused dog,' Raff said. 'He knows where Isaac lived but he can't get in. He's forming new bonds to you but his allegiance will be torn—he'll still want Isaac. And what's back there buried…who knows? Some long hidden loot, or a wombat hole, or something he sniffed on the way past and thought was worth investigating. But now… He's weighed everything up—you, wombats, Isaac—and decided he needs to go back to his first love.'

And Raff was right. They emerged from the bush and Kleppy was waiting for them—or rather he was waiting for someone to open the gate.

His nose was pressed hard against the cyclone fencing and he whimpered as they approached. He was no longer running. He was no longer joyful to see them.

Abby knelt and scooped him up and he looked longingly at the darkened house.

'He's not there any more,' she whispered, burying her nose into his scruffy coat. 'I'm sorry, Kleppy, but I'm it. Will I do?'

'He'll grow accustomed,' Raff said, and his voice was a bit rough—a bit emotional? 'You want me to take you both home?'

She looked at the darkened house, then turned and looked out towards the road, to where Ben had been snatched from her.

He'll grow accustomed.

Ten years…

Her parents would never forgive Raff Finn. How could she?

'It's okay, Kleppy,' she whispered. 'We'll manage, you and I. Thank you, Raff. We'd appreciate it if you took us home.'

He drove them down from the mountain, a woman and her dog, and he felt closer to her tonight than he had for ten years.

Maybe it was what she was wearing. The normally immaculate lawyer-cum-Abby was wearing old jeans, a faded sweatshirt and her hair had long come loose from its normally elegant chignon. She still had flour on her face from pasta making. There were twigs in her hair.

Her face was tear-streaked and she was holding her dog as if she were drowning.

She made him feel…

Like he'd felt at nineteen, when Abby had started dating Philip.

He and Abby had been girlfriend and boyfriend since they were fourteen and sixteen. Kid stuff. Not serious.

She hung round with Sarah so she was always in and out of the house. She was pretty and she laughed at his jokes. She was always…there.

Then he'd come home and she was dating Philip and the sense of loss had him gutted.

He should have told her how he felt then, only he'd been too proud to say, *Okay, Abby, wise choice, I know at seventeen you need to date a few people, see the world.*

He'd been too proud to say that seeing her and Philip together had made him wake up to himself. Had made him realise that the sexiest, loveliest, funniest, happiest, most desirable woman in the world was Abby.

He had known it. It was just… He thought he'd punish her a little. He and Ben had even been a bit cool to her—Ben had hated her dating Dexter as well.

They'd backed off. The night of the crash, where was Abby? Home, washing her hair?

Home, being angry with all of them.

That probably saved her life, but what was left afterwards…?

The sexiest, loveliest, funniest, happiest, most desirable woman in the entire world had been hidden under a load of grief so great it overwhelmed them all. Then she was hidden by layers of her parents' hopes, their fixation that Abby could make up for Ben, and their belief that Philip was the Ben they couldn't have.

He'd watched for ten years as the layers had built up, until the Abby he'd once known, once loved, had been almost totally subsumed.

And there was nothing he could do about it because he was the one who'd caused it.

He felt his fists harden on the steering wheel, so tight his knuckles showed white. One stupid moment and so many worlds shot to pieces. Ben and Sarah. And Abby, condemned to live for the rest of her life making up for his criminal stupidity.

'You know I once loved you,' he said into the night and she gasped and hugged Kleppy tighter.

'Don't.'

'I won't,' he said gently. 'I can't. But, Abby, if I could wipe away that night…'

'As if anyone could do that.'

'No,' he said grimly. 'And I know I have to live with it for the rest of my life. But you don't.'

'I don't know what you mean.'

'I mean you lost Ben that night,' he said. 'For which I'm responsible and I'll live with that for ever. But Ben was my mate and if he could see what's happening to you now he'd be sick at heart.'

There was a long silence. She wasn't talking. He was trying to figure out what exactly to say.

He had no right to say anything. He'd forfeited that for sure, but then…

Forget himself, he thought. Forget everything except the fact that Ben had been his best friend and maybe he needed to put what he was feeling himself aside.

Make it about Ben, he told himself. Abby hated him already. Saying what he thought Ben would say couldn't make things worse.

'Abby, your parents and Dexter's parents are thick as thieves,' he told her. 'They always have been. After the accident, your families practically combined. The Dexters had Philip. The

Callahans were left only with Abby. Two families, a son and a daughter. When Ben died you were about to go to university and study creative arts. Afterwards, Philip told you how sensible law was. Your mother told you how happy it'd make her to see you at the same law school as Philip. Philip's dad told you he'd welcome you into his law firm. And you just…rolled.'

'I did not roll,' she said but it was a whisper he knew didn't even convince herself.

'You used to wear sweaters with stripes. You used to wear purple leggings. I loved those purple leggings.'

Silence.

'I never saw you wear purple leggings after Ben died.'

'So I grew up.'

'We all did that night,' he said gravely. 'But, Abby, you didn't just leave behind childhood. You left behind…Abby.'

'If you mean I left behind stupidity, yes, I did,' she snapped. 'How could I not? All those years… *Keep away from the Finn boy. He's trouble.* That's what my mother said but I never listened. Not once did I listen and neither did Ben, and now he's dead.'

He couldn't answer that.

The car nosed its way down the mountain. He could drive faster. He didn't.

Keep away from the Finn boy.

He knew Ben and Abby had been given those orders. He even knew why.

His grandfather's drunkenness. His mother's lack of a wedding ring. His family's poverty.

The prissiness of Abby's parents, secure in their middle class home, with their neat front lawn and their nice children.

'I dunno about the Callahan kids.' He remembered Gran saying it when he was small as she tucked him into bed. 'You be careful, Raff, love. They don't fit with the likes of us.'

'They're my friends.'

'And they're nice kids,' his gran had said. 'But one day they'll move on. Don't let 'em break your heart.'

As a kid, he didn't have a clue what she was talking about.

He'd figured it out as he got older, but Ben and Abby never let it happen. They simply ignored their parents' disapproval and he was a friend regardless.

But for how long? If Ben hadn't died…would Abby have gone out with him again?

And now she was a defence lawyer and he was a cop. Never the twain shall meet.

Except she was staring ahead with eyes that were blind with misery and she was heading into a marriage with Dexter and he couldn't bear it.

'I'm not talking about us now,' he said, and it was hard to keep his voice even. 'As you say, we've both grown up and there's so much baggage between us there's never going to be a bridge to friendship. But I'm not talking about me either, Abby. I'm talking about you. You and Dexter. He's burying you.'

'He's not.'

'Mrs Philip Dexter. Where's the Abby in that equation?'

'Leave it.'

'You know it's true. Would Mrs Philip Dexter ever spend the night trawling Banksia Bay looking for a dog?'

'Of course she would.' She gulped. 'No. That is…I'll hang onto Kleppy from now on.'

'And if Dexter leaves the door open?'

'He won't.'

'Don't do it, Abby.'

'Butt out.' They were pulling up outside her house. She shoved the door open and hauled Kleppy out. She staggered a little, but straight away he was beside her, steadying her.

She was so…so…

She was Abby. All he wanted to do was fold her into his arms and hold her. Dog and all.

He'd had ten years to stop feeling like this. He thought he had.

One stupid night hunting a kleptomaniac dog and he was feeling just what he'd felt ten years ago. As if here was the half to his whole. As if something had been ripped out of him ten years back and this woman was the key to getting his life back.

This wasn't about him. It couldn't be.

'There are lots of guys out there, Abby,' he said in a voice that was none too steady. 'Guys who'd marry you in a heartbeat. Guys who'd love Kleppy. Don't marry Dexter.'

'Get out of my way.'

'You're better than this, Abby.'

'We've had this conversation before. Philip's better than any of us. He wasn't stupid. He's dependable.'

'He's boring. He doesn't like this town.'

'How can you say that? He lives for this town.'

'He spends his life criticising it. Making reasons why he should go to conferences far away. Where are you going on your honeymoon?'

'You're suggesting we should honeymoon at Mrs Mac's Banksia Bay's Big Breakfast?'

'No, but...'

'That's what I'd have done if I'd married you.'

Her words shocked them both.

If I'd married you...

The unsayable had just been said.

The unthinkable had just been put out there.

'Abby...'

'Don't,' she said and pushed and Kleppy got caught in the middle and yelped his indignation. 'Now see what you've done.'

Kleppy wagged his tail. Wounded to the core.

'Think about it,' he said, but softly, knowing he'd gone too far; he'd pushed into places neither of them could contemplate going.

'I've thought about it. Thank you very much for your help tonight.'

'Any time, Abby, and I mean that.'

'I've accepted all the help from you I'll ever accept.'

'You can't say that. What if you need help over the street in your old age? There I'll be in my fading cop uniform, all ready to hold up the traffic, and there you'll be with your pride and your walking frame. *Don't you stop the traffic for me, young man...*'

She gasped and choked, laughter suddenly surfacing at the image.

'That's better,' he said. 'Abby, can we be friends?'

Friends. She looked at him and the laughter faded. Her eyes were indescribably bleak.

'No.'

'Because of Ben?'

'Because of much, much more than that.'

'Don't go near the Finn boy. He's trouble?' he said.

'More than that, too,' she whispered. 'You know I... You know we...'

He didn't know anything, and he couldn't bear it. She was looking at him with eyes that were so bleak the end of the world must be around the corner, not the marriage of the year, Banksia Bay's answer to a royal couple—a wedding that had been planned almost since she was a baby.

She hesitated for just a fraction of a second too long and logic and reason and everything else he should be thinking flew straight out of the window.

He took her shoulders in his hands. He tugged her to him— dog included—and he kissed her.

One minute she was angry and confused, intending to wheel away and stalk into the house, dignity intact.

The next minute she was being kissed by Raff Finn and her dignity was nowhere.

Second time in two days? She felt as if her body had opened to this two days ago and she'd been waiting for a repeat performance ever since.

Only this wasn't a repeat performance. Tonight she'd been scared and lonely and emotional, remembering so much stuff that her head was close to exploding even before Raff's mouth met hers.

It was no wonder that when it did she couldn't handle it.

She liked control. She was a control girl. Her emotional wiring was neat and orderly.

His mouth touched hers and every single fuse blew, just like that.

Her circuits closed down and every one of the emotions she'd been feeling during the night was replaced, overridden by one gigantic wire that sizzled and sparked and threatened to blow her tidy existence right out of the water.

Raff Finn was kissing her.

She was kissing Raff Finn.

Or…maybe she wasn't kissing. She was simply dissolving into him.

Ten long years of control, ten years of carefully recreating her life, was forgotten. All she could feel was this man. His hands. His mouth. The taste of him, the smell, the sheer testosterone-laden charge of him.

Raff. The man who was kissing her totally, unutterably, mind-blowingly senseless.

She had sensations within her right now that she didn't know existed. She didn't know feeling like this was possible. If she had…

If she had, she'd have gone hunting for them with elephant guns.

Oh…

Did she gasp? Did she moan?

Who knew? All she knew was that her mouth was locked on his and the kiss went on and on and she didn't care. She didn't care that it was three in the morning and she was engaged to Philip Dexter and Raff Finn was a man her family hated. Raff Finn, six foot two, was holding her and kissing her until her toes curled, until her mind was empty of anything but the taste of him.

This was a pure primeval need. It had nothing to do with logic. It had everything to do with here and now. And Raff—a man she'd wanted since she was eight years old.

Here, now and…and…

'Is that you? Abigail?'

Uh-oh.

This was Banksia Bay.

It was three in the morning.

She lived next door to Ambrose Kittelty and Ambrose watched American sports television all night on Pay TV—as well as watching out of his front window.

Banksia Bay. Where her life was never her own. Could never be her own.

'It's Abby all right.' Somehow, Finn was putting her away from him and she could have wept. To have him so close... To know she could never... Must never...

'Is she kissing you?' Mr Kittelty sounded almost apoplectic.

'Bit of trouble with a dog,' Raff said smoothly. 'I'm helping the lady get him under control.'

'You looked like...'

'Took two of us to get him settled. Seems okay now. You right, ma'am?'

'That's Abrahams' dog,' Ambrose said.

'Yes, sir, the same dog that took your boot from the bowling club,' Finn said. 'Still causing trouble.'

'Get him put down,' Ambrose said and slammed down the window.

'I didn't know Ambrose and Phil were related,' Raff said and any last vestige of passion disappeared, just like that.

She felt cold and tired and stupid. Very, very stupid.

'Thank you for tonight,' she said, and she couldn't keep the weariness from her voice. 'Don't...'

'Come near you any more?'

'That's right,' she whispered. 'There's too much at stake.'

'Your marriage to Philip?'

'You know it's much more than that.'

'First things first, Abby,' he said softly. 'Figure the marriage thing out and everything else can come later.'

'Not with you, it can't.'

'I know that.'

'So goodnight,' she said and she hugged her dog close—a

wild dog this, he hadn't even wriggled while her brain had been short-circuiting—and she walked inside with as much dignity as she could muster.

She closed the door as if she was trying not to wake a household.

There was no household. Just Abby and Kleppy and one magnificent wedding dress.

'What will I do?' she whispered and she leaned back against the closed door. 'Kleppy, help me out here.'

Kleppy's butt wriggled until she set him on the floor. He headed into the bedroom while she stood motionless, trying not to think.

Kleppy headed straight back to her. Carrying her jewellery box.

He set it down at her feet and wriggled all over.

See? She had a guy who'd steal for her.

What more did a girl want?

Raff drove half a mile before he pulled over to the side of the road. He needed time to think.

He didn't have the head space to think.

Abby, Abby, Abby.

Ten years…

He'd been busy telling Abby she should move on. Could he?

He'd dated other women—of course he had. He'd set himself up with a life, of sorts. Living in this town. Keith, his partner, was getting long in the tooth. Keith was senior sergeant but, for all intents and purposes, Raff was in charge of the policing in this town. When Keith retired, Raff would be it.

Not bad for a Boy Who Meant Trouble.

He was still judged by some in this town, but only as someone whose background made people sniff, who'd been stupid in his youth. He was accepted as a decent cop. Sarah had friends, support groups, the farm she loved.

He had everything he needed in life, right there.

Except Abby.

How did you tell a woman you loved her?

He couldn't. To lay that on her... There was no way she could take it anywhere. They both knew that.

This thing between them...

He shouldn't have kissed her. It reminded him that it was more than a kid's dreaming. It was as real today as it had been the first time he'd kissed her. Life had been ahead of them, exciting, wonderful. Anything had been possible.

But to love Abby now...

She'd closed herself off. After Ben's death she'd simply shut down, retired into her parents' world, into Philip's world, and she'd never emerged. She was junior partner in Banksia Bay's legal firm. She was Philip's fiancée. Next Saturday she'd be Philip's wife.

The waste...

Do you want to marry her yourself?

The thought was enough to make him smile, only it wasn't a happy smile. He'd faced facts years ago. Even if she could shake off the past, to live with her parents' condemnation, with the knowledge that every time she looked at him she was seeing Ben...

They'd destroy each other.

A couple of kids drove past—Lexy Netherland driving his dad's new Ford. He bet Old Man Netherland didn't know Lexy was out on the tear. He had Milly Parker in the passenger seat. They'd be going up the mountain, to the lookout. Only not to look out.

Kids, falling in love.

He could put the sirens on, pull 'em over, send 'em home with their tails between their legs.

No way could he do that. It wasn't long before they'd be adults. The world would catch up with them and they'd be accepting life as it had to be.

As he had.

Loving Abby. Then Ben's death. Then the other side, where the woman he loved could never find the courage to move on.

He knew she was having doubts—how could he kiss her

and not sense it? Maybe if he pushed harder he could stop this marriage. But then what? What would he be doing to her?

He'd pushed her already to look seriously at the life she was facing. There was nothing else he could do. For Ben. For himself.

He put his head on the steering wheel and thumped it. Hard. Three times.

The third time he hit the horn and the dogs in Muriel Blake's backyard started barking to wake the dead.

Time to move on, then?

Back to Sarah.

Back home.

Where to move forward in this town?

There was never a forward.

CHAPTER NINE

How to sleep after a night like this? She did at last, but not until dawn. She woke and it was ten o'clock and she'd been meant to meet Philip for breakfast at the yacht club.

She phoned and he was fine.

'No problem. I have three newspapers and Don's here with his plans for the new supermarket. As long as it's safe and clean, I can do without my wallet until later. I've hardly realised you weren't here.'

That was supposed to make her feel better?

She showered slowly, washed her hair, took a long time drying it.

Kleppy watched, looking anxious.

'I'm not going anywhere today where I can't take you,' she told him. 'It's the weekend.'

He still looked anxious. He climbed onto her bed, and then onto the dressing table. Wriggled himself a spot next to her cedar box. His new favourite thing.

'I guess last night upset you,' she told him, abandoning her hairdryer to give him a hug. 'I'm so sorry about Isaac. It's horrid loving someone and losing them.'

Like she had.

Like Raff had.

It was Raff's fault.

But that mantra, said over and over in her head for ten years, sounded hollow and sad and bleak as death—a sentence stretched into the future as far as the horizon.

Could she put it away? Find the Raff she'd once loved?

Whoa. What was she thinking?

'It's wedding nerves,' she told Kleppy and on impulse she carried him into her spare room where her wedding gown hung in all its glory.

Two years of love had gone into making this dress.

She set Kleppy down. The little dog nosed his way around the hem, ducked under the full-circle skirt, poked his nose out again and headed back to her. She smiled and held him and stared at her dress some more.

She'd loved making this dress. Loved, loved, loved.

Once upon a time, this was what she was going to do. Sew for a living. Make beautiful things. Make people happy.

Now she was employed getting a low life off the hook. She was going to be Philip's wife.

But to draw back now...

The morning stretched on. She sat on the floor of her second bedroom and thought and thought and thought.

Her mother rang close to midday. 'You ready, darling?'

'Ready?'

'Sweetheart, don't joke,' her mother said sharply. 'This is your afternoon, like Thursday night was Philip's night. Philip's mother and I will be by to collect you in half an hour. Don't wear any of your silly dresses now, will you, dear. You know I hate them.'

Her silly dresses.

She meant the ones she'd made herself. The ones that weren't grey or black or cream.

This was a wedding celebration. Why not wear something silly? Polka dots. Her gorgeous swing skirt with Elvis prints all over?

'I'll drive myself,' she told her mother. 'I'll meet you at the golf club.'

'You won't be late?'

'When am I ever? Oh, and Mum?'

'What?'

'I'm bringing my dog.'

There was a moment's grim silence. Her mother would know what she was talking about. The whole town would know. She'd expected her mother to have vented her disapproval by now.

'Hasn't Philip talked some sense into you about that yet?'

'About that?'

'Abrahams' dog. Of all the stupid…'

'I'm keeping him.'

'Well.' Her mother's breath hissed in and Abby waited for the eruption. But then suddenly Abby could hear her smile. There was even a tinkling laugh. 'That's okay,' she said and Abby realised she was on speaker phone, and her mother was also talking to her father. 'Philip will cope with this.' Then, back to her… 'They don't let dogs in the club house.'

'They do on the terrace as long as I keep him leashed. It's a gorgeous day. I'm bringing him.'

'This is between you and Philip, not you and us,' her mother said serenely. 'Philip will talk you into sense, and we can cope with a dog for one afternoon. But don't be late. Isn't this exciting? So many plans, finally come together.'

She disconnected.

So many plans, finally come together.

Abby stood and stared at the phone. How could she do the unthinkable?

How could she not?

'I'm ready.'

Sarah looked beautiful. Hippy beautiful. There was a shop behind the main street catering for little girls who wanted to be fairies or butterflies and adults who wanted to be colourful. It suited Sarah exactly.

The woman who ran it thought Sarah was lovely. She rang Raff whenever a new consignment arrived and he'd wave goodbye to half his weekly salary. It was worth it. Sarah's joy in her pretty dresses and scarves and her psychedelic boots made up…well, made up in some measure for the rest.

She'd woken with another of her appalling headaches. It had

finally eased but she was still looking wan, despite her smile. Pretty clothes were the least he could give her.

'Can you drive me to the golf club now? I don't want to be late,' she said, anxious. She'd been looking forward to this week for months. Abby's pre-wedding parties. Abby's wedding itself.

'My car is at your disposal,' he said and pulled on his policeman's cap, tipping it like a chauffeur. She smiled.

'Tell me again why you're not coming.'

At least that was easy. 'It's girls only. I'd look a bit silly in a skirt.'

Sarah giggled, but her smile was fleeting. 'If it wasn't only girls, would you want to come?'

Sometimes she did this, shooting him serious, insightful questions, right when he didn't need them.

'Abby's mother doesn't like me,' he said, deciding to be honest. 'It makes things uncomfortable.'

'Because of the accident?'

'Yes.'

'Oh, Raff,' she said and walked over and hugged him. 'It's not fair.'

'There's not a lot we can do about it, Sares,' he told her and kissed her and put her away from him. 'Except be happy ourselves. Which we are. How can we help but be happy when you're wearing a bright pink and yellow and purple and blue skirt—and your purple boots have tassels?'

'Do you like them?' she said, giggling and twirling.

'I love them.'

He was making Sarah happy, he thought as they headed to the golf club to Abby's pre-wedding party. At least he could do that.

No one else?

No one else.

Philip was sailing. He'd gone out with his supermarket-planning mates. Even now he was cruising round Banksia Bay, discussing the pros and cons of investment opportunities.

How did you tell a guy you'd made the biggest mistake of your life when he was out at sea?

How did you go calmly to your pre-wedding party when you'd made a decision like this?

How did you call it off—when you hadn't told your fiancé first?

All those wedding gifts, coming her way. She'd be expected to unwrap them. Aargh.

But by now the gifts would already be in cars heading towards the golf club. It didn't make any difference if she said, *Don't give them to me today,* or if on Monday she re-wrapped them and sent them all back.

That'd be her penance. Sending gifts back.

That and a whole lot else.

She drove towards the golf club slowly. Very slowly. Kleppy lay beside her and even he seemed subdued. She turned into the car park. She sat and stared out through the windscreen, seeing nothing.

Someone tapped on her window. She raised her head and dredged up a smile. Sarah was peering in at her, looking worried.

'What's wrong? You look sad. Do you have another headache? Oh, Abby, and on your party day.'

Raff was right behind his sister. In civvies. Faded jeans and black T-shirt, stretched a bit too tight.

'No, I… I just didn't want to be the first to arrive.' She climbed from the car and sent Raff what she hoped was a bright smile, a smile that said she knew exactly what she was doing.

'Collywobbles?' he asked and it was just what she needed. It was the sort of word that made a woman gird her loins and stiffen her spine and send him a look that was pure defiance.

'Why on earth would I have collywobbles?'

'I'd have collywobbles if I was marrying Philip.'

'Go jump.'

'Philip's really handsome,' Sarah said. 'Almost as handsome as Lionel.'

'Lionel?' They said it in unison, distracted. They looked at each other. Looked back at Sarah.

'Lionel's cute,' Sarah said. 'So's your dress, Abby. I love the Elvises.'

'So do I,' Abby said, thinking she had one vote at least. She loved this dress—a tiny bustier, a full-circle skirt covered with Elvises—black and white print with crimson tulle underneath to make it flare. It was a party dress. A celebration dress.

What was she celebrating?

'And you've made Kleppy a matching bow.' Sarah scooped up the little dog and hugged him. 'He's adorable. He's even more adorable than Lionel.'

'Who's Lionel?' Abby asked.

'Kleppy's friend,' Sarah said simply. 'Ooh, there's Margy.' Abby's next door neighbour was pulling up on the far side of the car park, a dumpy little woman whose looks belied the fact that she ran the most efficient disability services organisation in the State. 'Hi, Margy. Can I sit next to you?' And she dived off, carrying Kleppy, leaving Abby and Raff together.

'Lionel?' she said, because that seemed the safest way to go.

'There's Lionel who was Isaac's gardener,' Raff said, frowning. 'I didn't realise he and Sarah knew each other, but Sarah gets around more than I think. Okay, have a great hen's party. I'll pick Sarah up at four.'

'Raff?'

'Yes?' He sounded testy.

She'd said his name. She needed to add something on the back of it. Something sensible.

But how to say what she needed to say? How to think about saying what she needed to say? How to get over the impossibility of even thinking about thinking about…?

Maybe she should stop thinking. Her head was about to fall off.

People were arriving all around them. Her friends. Her

mother's friends. Every woman in this little community who'd come into contact with her over the years seemed to be getting out of cars, carrying gifts into the golf club.

How many women had her mother invited?

How many gifts would she need to return?

'Abigail?' That was her mother calling. She was standing on the terrace, shielding her eyes from the sun, trying to see who her daughter was talking to. 'Your guests are here. You should be receiving them.'

'There you go,' Raff said and eased himself back into his car. 'By the way, I'm with Sarah. That's a cute dress. Really cute. You should try wearing that in court some time.'

'Raff?' She didn't want him to go. She didn't want…

'See you later,' he said.

He drove away. She stood there in her Elvis dress, staring after him like a dummy.

'Abigail.' Her mother's voice was sharp. 'What are you thinking? You're being discourteous to our guests. And what on earth are you wearing?'

A cute dress, she thought, as she headed up to her mother, to her waiting guests.

Abigail, what are you thinking?

What was he thinking?

Nothing. He'd better not think anything because if he did there was a chasm yawning and it was so big he couldn't see the bottom.

He needed some work. He needed a few kids to do something stupid so he could lay down the law, vent a bit of spleen, feel in control.

Abby in an Elvis dress.

Abby, who was marrying Philip.

Any minute now the steering wheel was going to break.

'Raff?' His radio crackled into life and he grabbed it as if it were a lifeline.

It was Keith. 'Yeah?'

'There's a bit of trouble down on the wharf. Couple of kids chucking craypots into the water, and Joe Paxton's threatening to do 'em damage. I'm stuck up on the ridge 'cos John Anderson's locked himself out. Can you deal?'

'Absolutely,' Raff said, feeling a whole heap better.

Trouble, he could deal with.

Just not how he was feeling about Abby.

The afternoon was interminable. She smiled and smiled, and thought she should have run. What was she thinking, letting this afternoon go ahead? Just because she needed to tell Philip first.

'You'll make such a lovely couple. A credit to the town.' That was Mrs Alderson, one of her mother's bridge partners. 'We're so looking forward to next Saturday.'

'Thank you,' she said and then realised that Mrs Alderson was carrying a rather long shoulder bag and something had peeped from the edge and Kleppy had just…just…

He was heading under the table, to the full length of his lead, looking satisfied.

She stooped to retrieve it. It was a romance novel, a brand she recognised. A really… Goodness, what was that on the front? She snatched it from her dog and handed it back, apologising.

Margot Alderson turned beet-red and stuffed it back into her bag.

'I don't know what you're doing with that dog,' she snapped. 'He's trouble. If you must get yourself a dog, get a nice one. I have a friend who breeds pekes.'

Kleppy looked up at her from under the table and wagged his tail. He'd done what he wanted. He'd had his snatch and he'd given it to his mistress.

'I kinda like Kleppy,' Abby said. 'And you know…I don't even mind a bit of trouble.'

Her mother's friend departed, still indignant. Abby stared after her, thinking—of all things—about the cover of the romance novel. The cover showed a truly fabulous hero, bare from the waist up.

I don't mind pecs, either, she added silently. *Or a bit of hot romance.*

He had two kids in the cells waiting for their parents to come and collect them. 'Take your time,' he'd told them. 'It'll do 'em good to sweat.

Which meant he was stuck at the station, babysitting two drunken adolescents. Forced to do nothing but think.

Abby.

A man could go quietly nuts.

It wasn't fair to interfere more than he already had.

He wasn't feeling fair.

'If I was a Neanderthal I'd go find me a club and a cave,' he muttered.

He wasn't. He was Banksia Bay's cop and Abby was a modern non-Neanderthal woman who knew her own mind. He had to respect it.

'I miss the old days,' he said morosely. 'It'd be so much easier to go set up a cave.'

It was over. The last gift was in her father's van, being taken home to their spare room, Abby's old bedroom, pink, pretty.

'I wish you'd come home for your last week,' her mother said, hugging her. 'It's where you belong.'

Abby said no, as she always said no. They left, leaving Abby sitting on the terrace with Kleppy.

Philip was coming by to meet her. She had to tell him.

Her mother's words... *It's where you belong.*

Where did she belong?

She didn't know.

'What do you mean you don't want to get married?'

To say Philip was gobsmacked would be an understatement. He was staring at her as if she'd lost her mind.

Maybe she had.

'I can't,' she muttered, miserable. She'd tried to get him to go for a walk with her, to get away from the people in the bar. He wouldn't. They were out on the terrace but they were still in full view.

Philip was tired from sailing. He didn't want a walk. He wanted to go home, have a shower, take a nap, then take his fiancée out to Banksia Bay's newest restaurant. That was what he'd planned.

He hadn't planned on Abby being difficult.

He hadn't planned on a broken engagement.

'It's just… Kleppy,' she said in a small voice and Philip stared at her as if she were demented.

'The dog.'

'He's made me…'

'What?'

What, indeed? She hardly understood it herself. How one dog could wake her from a ten-year fog. 'You don't like him,' she said.

'Of course I don't like him,' Philip snapped. 'He's a mutt. But I'm prepared to put up with him.'

'I don't want you to put up with him.' She took a deep breath. Tried to say what she scarcely understood herself. The thing in the middle of the fog. 'I don't want you to put up with me.'

'What are you saying?'

'You don't like me, Philip.'

He looked at her as if she'd lost her mind. 'Of course I like you. I love you. Haven't I shown you that, over and over? This is craziness. Pre-wedding nerves. To say…'

'You don't like this dress, do you?'

He stared down at the Elvises and he couldn't quite repress a wince. 'No, but…'

'And you painted your living room…our living room when I move in…beige. I don't like beige.'

'Then we'll paint it something else. I can cope.'

'See, that's exactly what I mean. You'll put up with something else. Like you put up with me.'

'This is nonsense.'

They were sitting at the table right on the edge of the terrace, with a view running all the way down the valley to the coast below. It was the most beautiful view in the world. If anyone looked out from the bar right now they'd see a man and a woman having a tête à tête, she flashing a diamond almost as wide as her finger, he taking her hand in his. Visibly calming down.

'Mum said this was bound to happen,' Philip said. 'She felt like this when she married my father. A week before the wedding. Pre-wedding jitters.'

Philip's mother. A mouse, totally dominated by Philip's father—and by Philip himself.

She'd seen Philip's mother looking at her dress today. Not brave enough to say she liked it. But just…looking.

'I don't want to be beige,' she whispered.

'You won't be beige. You'll be very happy. There's nothing you want that I can't give you.'

'I want you to like my dog.' She felt as if she was backed into a corner, trying to find reasons for the unreasonable. Trying to explain the unexplainable.

'I'll try and like your dog.'

'But why?' she said. 'There are women out there who like beige. There are women out there who don't like mutts. Why do you want to marry me?'

'I was always going to marry you.'

'That's just it,' she said and it was practically a wail. 'We've just drifted into this.'

'We did not drift. I made a decision ten years ago…'

'You wanted to marry me ten years ago?'

'Of course I did.' He sighed, exasperated. 'It's okay. I understand. One week of pre-wedding nerves isn't going to mess with ten years of plans.'

'Philip, I don't want to,' she said and, before she could think about being sensible, she hauled the diamond from her finger and laid it on the table in front of him. 'I can't. I know…I know it's sensible to marry you. You're a good man. I know you've been unfailingly good to me. I know you'll even put up with my dog and paint your living room sunbeam-yellow if I really want. But, you know what? I want someone who likes sunbeam-yellow.'

'What the…? Is there someone else?'

Someone else. At the thought of who that someone else was…at the sheer impossibility of saying his name, voicing the thought, her courage failed her. Her courage to say *Raff*.

But not her courage to do what she must, right now.

'I can't,' she said quietly. 'No matter what. This isn't about someone else, Philip. It's about what I'm feeling. Finding Kleppy… Yeah, it's crazy, but he makes me laugh. He's a little bit nuts and I love it. I wish you loved it. You don't, and it's made me see that I don't want to be Mrs Philip Dexter. You've been wonderful to me, Philip. You deserve a woman who thinks you're wonderful in return. You deserve a woman who'll love the life you want to live instead of putting up with it, and you deserve a woman who you'll think is wonderful instead of putting up with her.'

'Abby…' He was truly shocked now, ashen, and she felt dreadful. Appalling.

She had to do this.

She pushed the diamond closer to him, so close it nearly fell off the edge of the table.

Philip was a sensible man. This diamond was worth a fortune. He didn't let it fall. He took it, looked down at it for a long moment and then carefully zipped it into the pocket of his sailing anorak.

He rose.

'I'm damp in these clothes,' he said, pale and angry. 'I need to get changed. And you… You need to think about what you're throwing away. You're being foolish beyond belief. Insulting, even. I know it's pre-wedding nerves and I'll make allowances. Think about it overnight. I'll come and see you in the morning when you've had time to reconsider.'

'I won't reconsider.'

'You have twenty-four hours to see sense,' he snapped. 'After all I've done for you… I can't believe you'd be so ungrateful.

To walk away from me… Of all the crazy… Why don't you just get on a slow boat to China and be done with it?'

A slow boat to China? Right now, the concept had enormous merit, but she wasn't going anywhere.

She couldn't move. She sat and stared sightlessly over the golf course and she thought…nothing.

Someone came and cleared her glass. Asked if she'd like another drink. Asked if she and Philip were going to China for their honeymoon.

Finally let her be.

They'd be muttering in the bar. Wondering what she was doing, just sitting.

Expecting Philip to come back?

Maybe they'd seen his anger, his tight lips, his rigid stance as he'd stalked to his car.

Maybe the town already knew.

She wouldn't tell anyone. She couldn't. Philip had given her twenty-four hours to come to her senses. She owed it to him to wait, to make him see it was a measured, sensible decision.

Is there someone else?

She thought of Philip's demand. Was there?

Raff had kissed her. Twice. He'd made her feel…

She couldn't afford to acknowledge how he made her feel.

'Klep!' The call jolted her out of her misery, an unfamiliar voice filled with joy. It was one of the golf course groundsmen, striding up from the first tee. She looked closer and recognised him.

Lionel. Isaac's gardener. A big, burly man in his mid-thirties. Slow and sleepy and quiet.

He reached her and knelt on the terrace and Kleppy was licking his face with joy. 'Klep!'

'Lionel,' she said, hauling herself out of her introspection. 'What are you doing here?'

'Working,' he said, briefly extricating himself from Kleppy's licking. 'Gotta job mowing. Not as good as Mr Abrahams'. S'okay.'

'You and Kleppy are friends?'

'Yeah.'

Oh, help. She looked at the two of them and thought…and thought…

Thought they were greeting each other with a joy born of love.

'Did you want him?' It nearly killed her to say it. To lose Kleppy and Philip in the one afternoon…

She knew what would hurt most.

But… 'Can't,' Lionel said briefly. 'I live in a rooming house now. I had to sell the house when Baxter pinched Mum's money. Lost the house, then lost me job when Mr Abrahams died. Someone said the Finns had Klep. Went up there to see and Sarah said he were yours. Sarah said he were happy. You're looking after 'im?'

'I…yes.'

'He's a great dog, Klep,' Lionel said. 'Makes a man happy.'

'I… He'll make me happy.'

'Goodo,' Lionel said. 'That man… Dexter… They said you're getting married.'

'I…'

'He's the lawyer.' It wasn't a question.

'Yes.'

'He don't like dogs,' Lionel said. 'He come up to Mr Abrahams' when he made a will. Kleppy jumped up and it were like he was touching dirt. You and he…' He stopped, the question unasked. *You and he…*

'We'll sort it out,' Abby said. 'I love Kleppy enough for both of us.'

'That's good,' Lionel said. 'You've made me feel better. And you're a lucky woman. Kleppy's the best mate you could have.' He gave Kleppy a farewell hug and went back to mowing.

Abby kept on staring at nothing.

Like he was touching dirt…

She'd done the right thing. She didn't need twenty-four hours. *She was a lucky woman?*

Maybe she was. She had Kleppy and she was…*free?*

CHAPTER TEN

ABBY told no one but it was all over town by morning.

Abigail Callahan and Philip Dexter had had a row. She'd flung his ring back in his face. He'd accused her of having an affair. She'd accused him of having an affair. The wedding would cost squillions to cancel. Abby was threatening to go to China.

Abby was threatening to take the dog to China.

Why, oh, why, did she live in a small town?

The phone rang at seven-thirty and it was her mother. Hysterical.

'Sam Bolte said he saw you at the golf club and you weren't wearing your ring. I've just had a call from Ingrid. Ingrid says Sam says Philip was rigid with anger, and he said it's all about that stupid dog. Are you out of your mind?'

She laid back on the pillows and listened to her mother's hysteria and thought about it.

Was she out of her mind?

Kleppy was asleep on her feet.

She could sleep with Kleppy for ever. If she didn't do something about Raff.

She couldn't do something about Raff. There was nothing to do.

'It's okay, Mum, I'll sort it,' she said.

'Sort it? Tell Philip it's all a ghastly mistake? You know, if it means the difference between whether you marry or not, your father and I will even keep the creature.'

The creature nuzzled her left foot and she scratched his ear with her toe.

'That's really generous, but...'

'You can't cancel the wedding. It'll cost...'

'No, it won't.' This, at least, she could do. She'd figured it out, looked at the contract with the golf club, had it nailed. 'I lose my deposit, which is tiny. None of the food's been ordered. Nothing's final. I can do this.'

'You're never serious?'

'Mum, I don't want to marry Philip.'

There was a long, long silence. Then... 'Why not?' It was practically a wail.

'Because I don't want to be sensible. I like being a dog owner. I like that my dog's a thief.' She thought about it and decided, why not go for broke; her mother could hardly be any more upset than she was now. 'I might as well tell you... I don't think I want to be a lawyer, either.'

'You've lost your mind,' her mother moaned. 'John, come and tell your daughter she's lost her mind. Darling, we'll take you to the doctor. Dr Paterson's known you since you were little. He can give you something.'

'I'm not sure he can give me what I want.'

'What do you want?'

'My dog, for now,' she said, shoving another thought firmly away. 'My independence. My life.'

'Abigail...'

'I'm hanging up now, Mum,' she said. 'I love you very much, but I'm not marrying Philip and I'm not mad. Or I don't think I'm mad. I'm not actually sure who I am any more, but I think I need to find out, and I can't do that as Mrs Philip Dexter.'

'Rumour is she's thrown him over. Rumour is she met some guy at that conference she went to in Sydney last month. Chinese. Millionaire. Loaded. Couple of kids by a past marriage but that's not worrying her. Rumour is she wants to take the dog...'

Raff spent the morning feeling...
Surprised?

'Go away. I'm not home.'

She was pretending not to be home. The first couple of times the doorbell rang Kleppy barked, which might be a giveaway, but she fixed that. She tucked him firmly under the duvet, and she put her jewellery box down there with him. Which reminded her...

Should she give the box back to Philip's grandfather? He'd given it to her as a labour of love, on the premise she was marrying his grandson.

Maybe he was one of those out there ringing her doorbell, sent by her mother to tell her to be sensible.

It couldn't matter. Go away, go away, go away.

How long could she stay under the duvet? She started working out how much food she had in the place; when she'd be forced to do a grocery run. She thought of the impossibility of facing shopping in Banksia Bay. Maybe she and Kleppy could leave town for a bit.

Where could she go?

Somewhere Raff could find her. If he wanted to find her.

Don't think of that. Don't think of Raff. Get this awfulness out of the way, and then look forward. Please...

The doorbell rang again.

Go away.

It rang again, more insistent, and it was followed by a knock, too loud to be her mother. Philip?

Go away!

'Abigail Callahan?' The voice was stern with authority and it made her jump.

Raff.

Raff was right outside her front door.

Panic.

What did he think he was doing, hiking up to her front door as bold as brass? She peeked past the curtains and his patrol car was parked out front. With its lights flashing.

She practically moaned. This was all she needed. Who knew what the town was saying about her, but she did not need Raff in the mix. It was all too complicated.

Kleppy whined, sensing her confusion, and she hugged him and held her breath and willed Raff to go away.

But Raff Finn wasn't a man to calmly turn away.

'Abigail Callahan, I know you're in there. Answer the door, please, or I'll be forced to come back with a warrant.'

A warrant? What the…?

'Go away.' She yelled it to the front door and there was a moment's silence. And then a response, deep and serious, and only someone who knew him well could hear the laughter behind it.

'Miss Callahan, I'm here to inform you that your dog is suspected of petty larceny. I have information that stolen property may be being stored on your premises. Open the door now, please, or I'll be forced to take further action.'

Her dog…

Petty larceny…

She lifted the duvet and stared at Kleppy. Who gazed back, innocent as you please. What the…? He hadn't been out. How could he have stolen anything?

She'd given back her mother's friend's romance novel. Kleppy was clean.

'He hasn't done anything,' she yelled, and then had to try again because the first yell came out more like a squeak. 'Go find some other dog to pin it to. Kleppy's innocent.'

'There speaks a defence lawyer. Sorry, ma'am, but the evidence points to Kleppy.'

'What evidence?'

'Mrs Fryer's diamanté glasses case, given to her by her late husband. It's said to be worth a fortune, plus it has sentimental value. It's alleged it was stolen from her bag, which was parked underneath the table you were sitting at yesterday. I have reason to believe your dog was tied under that very table. Circumstantial, I'll grant you, but evidence enough for a warrant.'

Uh-oh.

She thought about it. Kleppy lying innocently at her feet through yesterday's lunch. A big table, twelve or so women. Twelve or so handbags at their respective owners' feet.

Uh-oh, uh-oh, uh-oh.

'I have more serious things to think about this morning than glasses cases,' she managed and she heard the laughter intensify.

'You're saying there's something more serious than grand theft?'

'I thought it was petty larceny.'

'That depends whether the diamantés are real. Mrs Fryer swears they are. I knew old Jack Fryer and I'm thinking otherwise but I need to give the lady the benefit of the doubt.'

'He hasn't got them,' she wailed. 'He'd have given them to me by now.'

'I need to search.'

'Go away.'

'Let me in, Abigail,' he said, stern again. 'The neighbours are looking.'

Oh, for heaven's sake. Raff walking in here… If anyone in this town got even the vaguest sniff of what she was feeling…of why she'd been jerked out of her miserable life into something resembling a future…

Her future.

The word somehow steadied her. She wasn't marrying Philip. She had a future. Okay, maybe she needed to step into it rather than hiding under the duvet.

She climbed out of bed and shrugged on her brand new honeymoon wrap. Where was her shabby pink chenille? She'd got rid of it. Of course she had. That was what a girl did when she was getting married.

So now she was stuck with pure silk. Pure silk and Raff. She shoved her toes into elegant white slippers, pasted a glower on her face and stomped through to the front door. Hauled it open.

Raff was there in his cop uniform. He looked…he looked…

Maybe how *he* looked wasn't the issue. 'Whoa,' he said, his gaze raking her from the toes up, and she felt herself start to burn. She'd had fun buying herself wedding lingerie. She'd never owned silk before. It was making her body feel…

Well, something was making her body feel—as if it had been a really bad idea to give all her shabby stuff to the welfare store. The way Raff was looking…

Stop it. She practically stamped her foot. Raff was a cop. He was here to search the place. What she was thinking?

She knew what she was thinking, and she'd better stop thinking it right now. Instead, she concentrated on keeping her glower at high beam and stood aside as he came in.

'I don't want you here.' What a lie.

'Needs must. You say you don't have a glasses case, ma'am?'

'If you say *ma'am* once more I may be up for copicide.'

'Copicide?'

'Whatever. Justifiable homicide. Kleppy didn't pinch anything.'

'Are you sure?'

She winced at that. 'Um… No.'

He grinned. 'Not such a good defence lawyer, then. So what's with the millionaire?'

'The millionaire?'

'The guy you've thrown Philip over for.'

The millionaire. If he only knew. 'I hate this town,' she muttered, and she didn't need to try and glower.

'So it's all a lie.'

'What's a lie?'

'That you've tossed Philip aside and found another.'

'Yes. No. I mean…'

He caught her hand and held it up for them both to see. She'd been wearing Philip's ring for two years now. A stark white band showed where the ring had been.

'Proof?' Raff said softly.

'If I ran off with someone else I wouldn't be here now,' she snapped. 'And if he was a millionaire I'd have a rock to match.'

'But you've given Philip the flick.'

'Philip and I are taking time to reassess our positions.'

He surveyed her thoughtfully, once more taking in the silk. 'That's lawyer speak for a ripper of a fight and no one's speaking. Does this mean Sarah and I get our pasta maker back?'

That was a punch below the belt. But still… The pasta maker and Philip, or no pasta maker and no Philip.

No choice.

How had she changed so much? This time last week she'd been the perfect bride. Now, here she was, standing in the hall with her criminal dog behind her, with Raff right here. Right in her hall. Big, sexy, smiling.

Raff.

'I'll check my bag,' she muttered but he put her aside quite gently.

'No, ma'am. I'll check your bag. I don't want evidence tampered with.'

'You're thinking of taking paw prints?'

He chuckled, a lovely rich sound that filled the hall; that made her feel…like there might be something on the far side of this awfulness.

Her bag was by the front door where she'd tossed it when she'd come in yesterday. Big, bright, covered with Elvises. She'd made it as a picnic bag, thinking wistfully her Elvis dress would look cute on picnics. As if Mrs Philip Dexter would ever go on picnics.

Now the bag was stuffed with legally gathered loot—all the small gifts she'd been given yesterday. These were the gifts she'd have to sort and send back, with a note saying very sorry, she wasn't marrying Philip.

She'd have to reword that. She wasn't sorry at all. Especially now Raff was here.

He squatted beside the bag and started laying gifts out on the floor.

'Candle holders—very tasteful. Place mats—a girl can't have too many place mats. What's with the Scent-O-Pine Air Freshener? Oh, that's from Mrs Fryer. She really doesn't like your Kleppy. Hey, His and Her key rings—very useful. Oh, and what's this?'

This was a glasses case. Exceedingly tasteful. Pink and purple, studded with huge diamantés.

'Worth a billion,' Raff said appreciatively. 'Every diamond over a carat, but not a one out of place. Lovely soft mouth, our villain.'

The villain had come to investigate, pushing his way through the crack in the bedroom door, nosing his way to the crime scene. Checking out the glasses case. Putting his paw on it, then looking back to Abby and wagging his tail.

'Don't say a thing, Klep,' Abby said. 'No admissions.'

'His DNA's all over it.'

'He put it on just now. He's as horrified as I am. And you… you've let the suspect himself contaminate the crime scene. I'm appalled.'

He grinned and rubbed Kleppy under the ear and Kleppy wriggled his tail, lifted the glasses case delicately from his hand and headed back into the bedroom. Straight under the duvet with the rest of his loot.

Raff looked through to the bedroom, thoughtful. 'Maybe I should search in there, too.'

'Don't you dare,' she said, suddenly panicking, and he straightened and his smile faded.

'I won't. You okay?'

'I'll live.'

'You have a hard few days ahead. I hope your millionaire's going to take care of you.'

'Raff…'

'Mmm?' He was watching her. Just…watching. The laughter had gone now. He was intense and caring and big and male and… and…

'I think I can put Ben behind me,' she said and his face stilled.

'Sorry?'

'I...'

How to say the unsayable? How to get it out? She'd never intended... In a few months, maybe, when the dust had settled... But now? Here?

'I think I might love you,' she whispered and the thought was out there—huge, filling the house with its danger.

Danger? That was what it felt like, she thought. A sword, hanging over her head, threatening to fall.

Falling in love with the bad boy.

'I know...this is dumb.' She was stammering, stupid with confusion. 'It's not the time to say it. I shouldn't... I mean, I don't know whether you want it. I'm not sure even that I want it, but I fell in love with you twenty years ago, Raff Finn, and I can't stop. This week...it's jolted me out of everything. It's made me see... Your craziness broke my heart but it hasn't changed anything. I can't... I can't stop loving you. If I can forgive what happened with Ben, is there a chance for us?'

'For us?' His face was emotionless. Still. Wary?

'Once upon a time we were boyfriend and girlfriend.' She hadn't got this right. She knew it but she didn't know how to get it right. 'I was hoping...'

'We might get together again?'

'Yes.'

'Now you've forgiven me.'

'I...yes. But...'

'There's no chance at all,' he said and suddenly there was no trace of laughter, no trace of gentleness, nothing at all. His voice was rough and cold and harsh. He looked stunned—and, unbelievably, he looked as if she'd just struck him. '*If I can forgive what happened to Ben...* What sort of statement is that?'

'It's what I need to do.'

'What do you mean?' he demanded.

'If I'm to love you. I need to forgive you if I'm to love you. All I'm saying is that I can. All I'm saying is that I think I have.'

Silence. Silence, silence and more silence.

She couldn't bear it. She wanted to dive back under the duvet and hide. Hide from the look on Raff's face.

But there was no escaping that look. There was such pain…

'There's no such thing as forgiveness for Ben,' he said at last, and the harshness was gone. It had been replaced with an emptiness that was even more dreadful. 'If you have to say it… It's still there.'

'Of course it's still there.'

'Of course,' he repeated. 'How can it not? And it always will be.' He took a deep breath. Another.

The silence was killing her.

She had this wrong. She didn't know how. She didn't know what she could do to repair it.

Would it ever be possible to repair it?

'Abby, ten years ago, I was crazily, criminally stupid,' he said at last, speaking slowly, emphasising each word as if it were being dragged out of him. 'I can't think about it without hating myself. But you know what? I've moved on.'

'You've…'

'If I hadn't, then I'd go insane,' he said. 'How do you think I felt? My best friend dead, my sister irreparably injured, and me with no memory of it at all. I was gutted by Ben's death—I still am. To lose such a friend… To inflict such pain on everyone who loved him… And more, every time I look at Sarah I know what I've done. But after ten years…'

Another deep breath. Another silence.

'After ten years, I have it in perspective,' he said. 'I've seen a lot of stupid kids. A lot of appalling accidents. There's always a driver; it's always someone's fault. But in those situations, you know what? There are other things, too. Kids egging other kids on. Being dumb themselves. That night Ben wasn't wearing a seat belt. We had 'em fitted—my gran insisted on it. Sarah wasn't wearing a seat belt, either—she was wearing a cute new dress she knew would crush. None of us should have been up there on that track in the rain. It was totally dumb. Yes, I was driving. Yes, I must have veered to the wrong side of the road and Philip says I was speeding. I've taken that on board. I've convicted myself and I've received my sentence. I've lost Ben as you've lost Ben. I've lost parts of Sarah, and my actions hurt so many, had so many repercussions, they can never be repaired. That's what I live with, Abby, every day of my life, and I'm not adding to it.'

'I don't…I don't know what you mean.'

'If we took this further… Waking up every morning beside a woman who says she forgives me? What sort of sentence it that? This week…okay, I've kissed you and yes, I've wanted you. I've given you a hard time about marrying Philip. And you know what? Last night, when the whispers went round that you'd given back his ring, for one breathtaking moment I thought maybe we could figure out some sort of future. But now… You forgive me? Graciously? Lovingly? Thanks, but no thanks. I can't live with that, Abby. You do what you need to do, but don't factor me in. Fetch Mrs Fryer's glasses case, please. I need to go.'

'Raff…'

'Don't push this any further,' he snapped. 'Figure it out for yourself. It's your life. I've done what I need to survive and forgiveness doesn't come into it. Acceptance…that's a much harder call.'

She stared up at him, confused. Shattered. Knowing, though…knowing in the back of her mind that he was right.

She forgave him?

Where was a future in that?

Raff returned the glasses case to Mrs Fryer, who took it with suspicion and examined it from all angles for damage. She glared at him and he thought that if it had been his dog that had taken the case, he'd be up on charges by now. Even though the case was worth zip.

Diamonds? He'd seen a diamond that big and he knew what a real one looked like. That diamond was sitting in Philip's security safe by now, he thought. That it wasn't sitting on Abby's finger...

He couldn't afford to go there.

'Did you see her?' Mrs Fryer hissed.

'See who, ma'am?'

'Abigail.'

'I did. She's extremely apologetic. I believe she may come round later and apologise in person.'

'Was there anyone with her?'

'Her dog,' Raff said neutrally and Mrs Fryer sighed in exasperation.

'No, dummy. I mean a man. Is there anyone else?'

'I believe the crime was the dog's own work,' Raff said, and turned and left before Mrs Fryer could slap him.

Anyone else...

No. Only him. She'd tossed Philip's ring back at him because she loved...*him?*

I think I might love you.

The words echoed over and over in his head. Where did a man go with that?

Without thinking, he found himself driving past his little farm, further up the mountain, up near Isaac's place, to the road where one night ten years ago his world had been blasted to bits.

How long did a man suffer for one moment's stupidity?

He'd stopped suffering. Almost. He'd almost found peace. Until Abby had said...

I think I might love you.

He couldn't afford to let her words rip him apart. He had his life to get on with and she had hers.

It might be a good idea if she did go to China.

CHAPTER ELEVEN

ON SUNDAY afternoon Abby decided that she did need to speak to Philip. It was only fair. What followed was a very stilted phone call. Philip sounded appalled and angry and confused. She crept back under her duvet and hugged Kleppy and decided she didn't need milk or bread; she could live on baked beans for a while.

The whole town was judging her.

On Monday she decided she couldn't hide under her duvet for ever. She had to pull herself together. She was not a whimpering mess. She was not hiding a millionaire under her bed. She needed to get on with her life.

That meant getting out of bed, dressing as she always dressed, smart and corporate for the last time. Today she'd wind up this court case with Philip and then she'd resign. She'd talk reasonably to her parents. She'd start sending gifts back and then figure, slowly and sensibly, where she wanted to take her life from here.

She did need to be sensible. She no longer wanted to be a lawyer, but that didn't mean stranding Philip or stranding her clients without reasonable notice. That was the sort of thing an hysterical ex-bride would do—the sort of woman who'd throw Philip over for some crazy, unreasonable love.

She wasn't that woman. She'd ended an unsuitable engagement for totally sensible reasons and she was totally in control. She entered court with her head held high. She sat in court and concentrated on looking…normal.

She was aware that the courthouse held more people than it had on Friday. That'd be because people were looking at her. The woman who ditched Philip Dexter.

No matter. She was in control. Kleppy was safely locked up. She looked neat and respectable, and her court notes were beautifully filed in her lovely Italian briefcase in the order they were needed.

As the morning stretched on, she decided she hated her briefcase. She'd give it back to Philip, she thought. That was sensible. He might find a use for a matching pair.

Back home, her wedding dress was packed in tissue, waiting for someone to make another sensible decision.

What to do with two thousand beads?

Decisions, decisions, decisions.

She concentrated on taking notes for Philip, handing him the papers he needed, keeping on her sensible face—but it was really hard, and when Raff entered the courtroom she thought her face might crack. Quite soon.

Philip had called Raff back on a point of law. Just clarifying the prosecution case. Just decimating the case Raff had put together with such care.

Raff wasn't a lawyer and he had no help. The Crown Prosecutor was hopeless. She wanted to cross the room and shake him, but Malcolm was eighty and he looked like if she shook him his teeth would fall out or he'd die of a coronary.

Wallace Baxter would get off. She could hear it in Philip's voice.

Philip might not have had a very good weekend—yes, his fiancée had jilted him—but there was nothing of the destroyed lover in his bearing. As the morning wore on he started sounding smug.

He was winning.

He sat down beside her after pulling the last of Raff's evidence apart and he gave her a conspiratorial smile.

He didn't mind, she thought incredulously. He didn't mind that she'd thrown back his ring—or not so much that it stopped him enjoying winning.

Her sensible face was slipping.

'This is brilliant,' Wallace hissed beside her. 'Philip's great. The stuff he's done to get me off… But what's this I hear about your engagement being off? You'd be a fool to walk away from a guy this great.'

A guy this great. Wallace was beaming.

She felt sick.

She stared around to the back of the court where Bert and Gwen Mackervale looked close to tears. Because of Wallace Baxter's deception they'd had to sell their house. They were living in their daughter's spare bedroom.

She thought of Lionel, a lovely, gentle man who'd live in a rooming house for ever. Because of Wallace.

And because of Philip's skill in defending him.

She looked at Wallace and Philip and the smile between them was almost conspiratorial. The vague suspicions she'd been having about this case cemented into a tight knot of certainty. *The stuff he's done to get me off…*

She was lawyer for the defence. Sensible defence lawyers did not question their own cases.

She'd stopped being sensible on Saturday afternoon. Or she thought she had. Maybe there was more *sensible* she had to discard.

She looked at Wallace—a guy who'd systematically cheated for all his life. She looked at Philip, smug and sure.

She looked at Raff, who'd lost control of a car one dark night when he was nineteen years old.

Forgive?

'It's nailed,' Philip said. 'Let's see Finn get out of this.'

Finn get out of this?

Wallace, surely.

But she looked at Philip and she knew he hadn't made a mistake. Morality didn't come into it. Raff was on the other side, therefore Raff had to be defeated.

How could she ever have thought she could marry Philip? How could her life have ended up here?

Her head was spinning. Define sensible? Sitting in a Banksia Bay courtroom defending Wallace Baxter?

Wallace and Philip…smug. Winning.

Wallace and Philip… *The stuff he's done to get me off*…

Her thoughts were racing, suspicions surfacing everywhere. She didn't know for sure, but in Philip's briefcase… The briefcase that matched hers…

What was she thinking?

Raff was leaving now, his evidence finished. She could see by the set of his shoulders that he knew exactly what would happen.

He'd done his best for the town—for a town that judged him.

Wallace was smiling. Philip was smiling. There were only a couple of minor defence witnesses to go and then summing up. Unless…unless…

She couldn't bear it.

Philip. Smiling. The model citizen.

Raff. Grim and stoic. The bad boy.

She was a mess of conflicting emotion. She was trying to get things clear but it was like wading into custard. All she knew was that she couldn't stay here a moment longer.

'Excuse me,' she said to the men beside her. 'I need to go.'

'Where?' Philip said, astounded.

'To check on Kleppy. He gets into trouble alone.'

'You can't walk out—to check on a dog.'

'No,' she said. 'Not just to check a dog. Much, much more.'

She rose and the eyes of the court were on her. Too bad. She wasn't sure what she was doing, but there was no way in the world she could sit here any longer.

'Bye,' she said, to the courtroom in general.

'Don't be stupid,' Philip snapped, and she looked at him for a long moment and then she shook her head.

'I won't. Not any more. Bye, Philip.'

She lifted up the glossy Italian briefcase from under the desk, swiftly checking she had the right discreet initials, and she strode out of the court. Her pert black shoes clicked on the floor as she walked, and she didn't look back once.

Raff paused in the entrance, to take a few deep breaths, to think there was no one to punch.

He'd wanted to punch Dexter for maybe ten years. He couldn't. Good cops didn't punch defence lawyers. Dexter was just doing his job.

Another deep breath.

'Raff.'

He turned and Abby was closing the courtroom door. Leaning against it. Closing her eyes.

'Hey,' he said and she opened her eyes and met his gaze. Full on.

'Hey.' She sounded like someone just waking up.

'You taking a break?'

'I need to go home and check Kleppy.'

'Fair enough.' He hesitated. Thought about offering her a ride. Thought that might be a bad idea.

Her sports car was close, in the place marked *Abigail Callahan, Solicitor*. Her spot was closer than the one marked *Police*. It wasn't as close as Dexter's though. Dexter and the Judge had parking spaces side by side.

Dexter's Porsche was the most expensive car in the car park.

Get through the other side of anger, he told himself harshly. Was there another side?

Abby had passed him now, walking into the sunlight to her car. She raised her briefcase to lay it in the passenger seat.

Hesitated.

She lowered her briefcase. Fiddled with the catch.

Raised it again. Tipped.

Papers went everywhere, a sprawl of legal paperwork fluttering in the sunlight. And tapes. A score of tiny audio cassettes.

'Whoops,' she said as tapes went flying.

The Abigail Callahan he'd known for the last ten years would never say *whoops*.

But she didn't look fussed. She didn't move. She didn't begin to pick anything up.

He didn't move either. He wasn't sure what was going on.

'You know, these should probably be picked up,' she said. 'They might be important.'

Might they?

'I'm sorry to trouble you, but I seem to have taken the wrong briefcase,' she said, sounding carefully neutral. 'But I'm in such a hurry… Would you mind putting the stuff back in and returning it to Philip?'

What the…?

'There's no rush,' she continued. 'Philip has his notes on the desk so he won't miss these for a while. Maybe you could go back to the station to sort them into order before you give them back. I'm sure Philip would think that was a kindness.'

She sighed then, looking at the mess of tapes and paperwork. 'This is what comes of having matching briefcases,' she said. 'They're so easy to mix up. I told Philip it was a bad idea—I did want a blue one. But at least I do know this is Philip's—because of the tapes. Philip always records his client appointments. He's a stickler for recording…everything. He always has. My briefcase holds files for submission to court. Philip's files and tapes are always in much more detail.'

They stood staring at each other in the sunlight. Abby…

'The tapes, Raff,' she said gently, and she gave him a wide, impudent smile. It was a smile he hadn't seen for years. It made him feel… It made him feel…

As if Abby was back.

'You'll take care of them?' she asked.

'I…yes.' What else was a man to say?

'Have fun, then,' she said and she climbed into her car. 'I'm sure you will.'

He collected the tapes with speed—something told him it might be important to have them collected and be gone before Dexter realised the mix-up.

He thought about Abby.

He headed back to the station thinking about Abby.

Life was getting…interesting.

Have fun?

He should be thinking about tapes.

He was, but he was also thinking about Abby.

She went home, but only briefly. She changed into jeans, collected Kleppy and headed up the mountain.

She had some hard thinking to do, and it seemed the mountain was the place to do it. For a little bit she thought about Philip's briefcase but by the time she reached the mountain she'd forgotten all about Philip. She'd moved on.

She parked out the front of Isaac's place—the safest place to park. Kleppy whined against the fence and she cuddled him and thought…

Ben was here.

That was why she'd come. Ben had died up here, in the thick bushland on the mountain, a place that had magically been spared logging, where the gums were vast and the scenery was breathtaking. After all these years, suddenly it felt right that she was here with him. Her brother.

For the last ten years Ben had been lost, and she'd been empty.

With Kleppy carefully on the lead—who knew what he'd find here?—she walked along the side of the road where the crash had happened. The smells were driving Kleppy wild. He tugged to the place he'd been digging the night she and Raff had been here, but she pulled him away.

'No wombat holes,' she told him. 'Sorry, Klep, but this trip is about me.'

She reached the foot of the crest. The road was incredibly narrow. The trees were huge—they were so close to the road.

Two cars colliding at speed… They'd never stood a chance.

She thought of that night. Of how they'd been before. Five kids. Fledgling love affairs. The things they'd all done.

Stupid kids, trying their wings. They'd been so sure they could fly. The only unknown was how far.

They'd been kids who thought they were invincible.

One stupid night.

She sank onto the verge at the side of the road and hugged her dog. 'Raff's right,' she whispered, the emotions of the past two days kaleidoscoping and merging into one clear vision. 'To forgive… That means he was wrong; the rest of us were right. That's how we've acted and that's what he's worn. He's accepted total blame.'

How hard must that have been?

A truck was approaching, slowly, a rattler. It came over the crest and slowed and stopped.

Lionel. Climbing out. Looking worried. 'Are you okay?' he asked.

Then he saw Kleppy and Kleppy saw him. It was hard to say who was most delighted and it took a while before Lionel finally told her why he was here.

'I keep coming up hoping she's left the gate open,' Lionel told her. 'Mr Isaac's daughter. She's locked the place and I can't water the spuds. We were growing blue ones this year, just to see what they're like.'

'It's a lovely garden.'

'It was a lovely garden,' he said, sad again, and he gave Kleppy a final hug and rose. 'The gate's still shut?'

'Yes.'

'I'd better slope off then,' he said sadly. 'Back to the golf course.' He sighed and glanced towards the garden. 'You gotta put stuff behind you. I'll be good at growing grass.'

'You will, too.'

'I might go out to see Sarah some time,' he said diffidently. 'You be out there, too?'

'I…probably not. I'm not sure.'

'You're Sarah's friend?'

'I am.'

'And the copper's friend? Raff?'

'I hope so.'

'He's good,' Lionel said. 'When I wanted to keep Kleppy he came to see my landlady; told her how much I wanted him. Didn't make any difference but he tried. I reckon a man like that's a friend.'

'He…he is.'

'And I bet he's pleased Kleppy's found you,' Lionel said, and he hugged Kleppy one last time and headed off back to his golf course.

She sat on the verge with her dog for a while longer. Letting her thoughts go where they willed.

She fiddled with the medal on Kleppy's collar. Thought about Lionel. Thought about Isaac.

Isaac Abrahams was a brave man, she thought. He'd been through so much—and he'd gone through more for his dog.

And Raff?

He'd faced condemnation from this community from the time he was a kid, and after Ben's death it had been overwhelming. He'd been based in Sydney at the Police Training College when the accident happened. All he'd needed to do to escape censure was move Sarah into a Sydney apartment and never come back.

He'd come back and faced condemnation because this was the place Sarah loved.

What you did for love…

She hugged her dog and looked at his collar and thought about what brave meant.

And what forgiveness was.

Tears were slipping down her cheeks now and she didn't care. These tears should have been cried out years ago, only she'd shut them out, shut herself down, turned into someone who couldn't face pain.

Turned into someone she didn't like.

Could Raff like her?

In time. Maybe. If she changed and waited for a while.

But then she thought about the expression on his face as she'd told him.

If I can forgive what happened with Ben…

How could she have said it? How could she be so hurtful?

Kleppy whined and squirmed and she hugged him tighter than he approved. She let him loose a little and he licked her from throat to chin. She chuckled.

'Oh, Kleppy, I love you.'

Love.

The word hung out there, four letters, a concept huge in what it meant.

Love.

She whispered it again, trying it out for size. Thinking of all its implications.

Love.

'I love Raff,' she told Kleppy, and Kleppy tried the tongue thing again.

'No.' She set him down and rose, staring along the track where Ben had died. 'I love you, Kleppy, but I love Raff more. Ben, I love Raff.'

Was it stupid to talk to a brother who'd been dead for ten years? Who knew, and it was probably her imagination that a breeze rustled through the trees right then, a soft, embracing breeze that warmed her, that told her it was okay, that told her to follow her heart.

'Just as well,' she told her big brother in a tone she hadn't used for ten years. 'You always were bossy but you can't boss me out of this one. I love Rafferty Finn. I love Banksia Bay's bad boy, and there's nothing you or anyone else can do to change my mind.'

CHAPTER TWELVE

THE sight of Wallace Baxter's face as the Crown Prosecutor asked a seemingly insignificant question about a bank account in the Seychelles was priceless.

As Crown Prosecutor, Malcolm might be too tired to do hard research, but when something was handed to him on a plate he shed twenty years in twenty seconds. Raff slipped him a question with a matching document, and suddenly Malcolm was the incisive legal machine he'd once been.

Wallace Baxter was heading for jail. The people he'd ripped off might even be headed for compensation.

And there'd be more, Raff thought with grim satisfaction. Raff had spent half an hour with Keith, poring through documents, listening to snatches of conversation, before Raff found the Seychelles document and they knew they had enough to pin Baxter.

They also suspected this was the tip of an iceberg. Philip's tapes might have been intended for blackmail, or maybe they were simply a product of an obsessive mind, but they covered this case only, and there'd been murky cases in the past. By the time Philip finished in court there'd be forensic investigators on his doorstep, Raff thought with satisfaction. With search warrants.

Keith, though, was in charge at that end. He was calling for backup. Raff's role was to return to court, focusing on this case only. So he listened to Malcolm ask his question and wave bank statements. He saw the moment Philip realised Abby had taken the wrong briefcase, and he watched his face turn ashen.

What had Philip been thinking, to record everything? Who knew? All he knew was that he was very, very pleased Abby was no longer marrying him.

He wanted to find her, but that was stupid. Wanting Abby had been stupid last night and it was stupid now.

He could leave the case to Malcolm now. He left. He should go back to help Keith—but he didn't. Instead, he stopped at the baker's to buy lamingtons. Sarah's favourite. They'd sit in the sun and eat them, he thought. He needed to settle.

But when he got home he remembered Sarah was at the sheltered workshop on Mondays. What was he thinking, to forget that?

Maybe he'd been thinking about why he couldn't go find Abby.

Stupid, stupid, stupid.

Should he go back and help Keith?

Keith would do just fine without him—and for some reason he didn't want to see the grubby details of Philip's profit-making. He didn't want to think about Philip.

Instead, he turned his attention to the garden. There was plenty here that needed doing. His grandmother would break her heart if she could see how he'd let it run down.

This was a gorgeous old house, but huge. There were four bedrooms in the main house and there was another smaller house at the rear where he and Sarah had lived with their mother before her death, to give them some measure of independence.

Sarah would like to live there now. She hankered for independence but she couldn't quite manage. She loved it here, though. To move away...

He couldn't, even if it meant spending his spare time mending and mowing and tending animals and feeling guilty because his grandmother's garden was now mostly grass.

And he was too close to Abby.

Do not go there, he told himself. He started tugging weeds, but then…

The sound of a car approaching tugged him out of his introspection.

Abby.

The car door opened and Kleppy flew to greet him as if he was his long lost friend, missing at sea for years, feared dead, miraculously restored to life. This was the new, renewed Kleppy, sure again of his importance in the world, greeting friends as they ought to be greeted.

He grinned and scratched Kleppy's stomach as he rolled, and Kleppy moaned and wriggled and moaned some more.

'I wish someone was that pleased to see me,' Abby said.

She was right by her car. She was smiling.

He couldn't roll on his back and wriggle but the feeling was similar.

She'd been crying. He could see it. He wanted…he wanted…

To back off. What she'd said… *If I can forgive what happened with Ben…* He'd gone over it in his mind a hundred times and he couldn't get away from it.

He could not afford to love this woman.

'I came to apologise,' she said.

He stilled. Thought about it. Thought where it might be going and thought a man would be wise to be cautious.

'Why would you want to apologise?' He rose. Kleppy gave a yelp of indignation. He grinned and scooped Kleppy up with him. Got his face licked. Didn't mind.

Abby was apologising?

'The forgiveness thing,' she said, and he could see it was an effort to make her voice steady. 'I didn't get it.'

'And now you do?'

She was standing beside her little red sports car and she wasn't moving. He didn't move either. He held her dog and he didn't go near.

Neutral territory between them. A chasm…

'I've…changed,' she said.

He nodded, still cautious. 'You got rid of the diamond. That's got to be a start.'

'It wasn't the diamond. It was Kleppy. One dog and my life turns upside down.'

'He hasn't ended you in jail.'

'Not yet.'

'How much did you know about what was in Dexter's briefcase?'

'Was there anything?' She couldn't disguise the eagerness. She didn't know, he thought with a rush of relief, though he'd already felt it. The Abby he once knew could never have collaborated with dishonesty. She hadn't changed so much.

Maybe she hadn't changed very much at all. This was the Abby he once knew, right here.

'There's enough to convict Baxter,' he said mildly—there was no need to go into the rest of it yet—and he watched the rush of relief.

'I'm so glad.'

'So are a lot of people. Me included. Is that why you're here? To find out?'

'No. I told you. I came to say sorry.'

Sorry. What did that mean?

He couldn't help her. He knew she was struggling, but she had to figure for herself where she was going.

Abby.

He wanted to walk towards her and gather her up and claim her, right now. He ached to kiss away the tracks of those tears.

But he had to wait, to see if the figuring would come out on his side.

'Kleppy and I have been up at Isaac's,' she said. 'We've been sitting on the road where Ben was killed.'

'Mmm.' Nothing more was possible.

'We were all dumb that night.'

'We were.' Still he was neutral. He was having trouble getting a breath here. Abby took a deep breath for him.

'Sarah and I were seventeen. You and Ben and Philip were

nineteen. I'd made my debut with Philip and you were mad at me. Sarah was mad at you, so she accepted a date with Philip to make you madder still. Ben was fed up with all of us—I think he wanted to go out with Sarah so he was fuming. Then the car... The rain... It would have been far more sensible to wait till the next weekend but Ben had to go back to uni so he was aching to try the car.'

'Abby...'

'Let me say it,' she said. 'I'm still trying to figure this out for myself so let me say it as I see it now.'

'Okay.' What else was a man to say?

'My dad came up here that afternoon and he was angry with Ben for spending the weekend here and not sitting in our living room giving Mum and Dad a minute by minute description of life at uni. So Dad didn't take any interest. He should have said, *Don't try the car until next weekend.* Or even offered to go with you and watch. And Sarah... I remember her trying on the dress I'd just finished making for her, and your gran saying, "Don't you crush that dress, Sarah, after all the time I spent ironing it." And I was home, fed up with the lot of you.'

'So...'

'So it was all just...there,' she said. 'Pressure on you to drive on a night that wasn't safe. Excitement. Knowledge that no one used that track except loggers and no loggers worked over the weekend. Stupid kids and unsafe decisions and a slippery road, and pure bad luck. Sarah not wanting to crush her dress. Ben being too macho to wear a seat belt. Philip wanting to show off his car, his girlfriend. You weren't charged with culpable driving, Raff, and there was a reason. My parents took their grief out in anger. Their anger soured...lots of things. It enveloped me and I've been too much of a wuss to fight my way out the other side.'

'And now you have?' It was a hard question to ask. It was a hard question to wait for an answer.

But it seemed she had an answer ready. 'You kissed me,' she said simply. 'And it made me realise that I want you. I always have. That want, that need, got all mixed up, buried, subsumed by grief, by shock, by obligation. I've been a king-sized dope, Raff. It took one crazy dog to shake me out of it.'

The dog in question was passive now, shrugged against Raff's chest. Raff set him down with care. It seemed suddenly important to have his arms free. 'So you're saying…'

'I'm saying I love you,' she said, steadily and surely. 'I know it seems fast. We've been apart for ten years so maybe I should gradually show you I've changed. But you know what? I can't wait. I've messed the last ten years up. Do I need to mess any more?'

He didn't move. He didn't let himself move. Not yet. There were things that needed to be said.

'Your parents hate me,' he said at last, because it was important. Hate always was.

'They have a choice,' she said steadily now, and certain. Her eyes not leaving his. 'They can accept the man I love or not. It's up to them but it won't stop me loving you. I'll try and explain but if they won't listen…' She took a deep breath. 'I can't live with hate any more, Raff, or with grief. I can't live under the shadow of a ten-year-old tragedy. You and me…' She gazed round the disreputable farmyard. 'You and me, and Sarah…'

And Sarah? She was going there?

She'd accept Sarah. He knew she would.

He could never leave Sarah. That fact had coloured every relationship he'd had since the accident, but this was the old Abby emerging, and it was no longer an issue. This was the Abby who held to her friendships no matter what, who'd never stopped loving Sarah, the Abby with a heart so big…

So big she could ignore her parents' hatred?

So big she could take on the Finn boy?

And then he paused. Another vehicle was approaching, travelling fast. Its speed gave it a sense of urgency and he and Abby paused and waited.

It was a silver Porsche.

Philip.

* * *

For ten years Abby had never seen Philip angry. She'd seen him irritated, frustrated, condescending. She'd always felt there was an edge of anger held back but she'd never seen it.

She was seeing it now. His car skidded to a halt in a spray of gravel, and the hens clucking round the yard squawked and flew for cover. Kleppy dived behind her legs and stayed there.

Philip didn't notice the hens or Kleppy. He was out of the car, crashing the door closed, staring at her as if she were an alien species.

Raff was suddenly beside her. Taking her hand in his. Holding her against him.

Uh-oh.

She should pull away. Holding hands with Raff would inflame the situation.

She tugged but Raff didn't let her go. Instead, he tugged her tighter. His body language was unmistakable. My woman, Dexter. Threaten her at your peril.

How had it come to this?

'So that's it,' Philip snarled, staring at the pair of them as if they'd crawled from under Raff's pile of weeds. 'You slut.'

'It's not polite to call a lady a slut,' Raff said and his body shifted imperceptibly between them. 'You want to take a cold shower and come back when you're cooler?'

'You sabotaged the case,' Philip said incredulously, ignoring Raff. 'The bank accounts… Suddenly you leave, and my briefcase's gone and in comes Finn and the Prosecutor has a whole list of new evidence. *You gave it to Finn.*'

'Baxter's a maw-worm,' Abby said, trying to shove Raff aside so she could face him. This was her business, not Raff's. 'I didn't know there was anything in your briefcase to convict him, but if there was we shouldn't have been defending him.'

'It's what we do. Do you know how much his fee was?'

'We can afford to lose it.'

'You might.' He was practically apoplectic, and she knew why. She'd had the temerity to get between him and his money. Philip and his reputation. Philip and his carefully planned life.

'So what about this?' He hauled the diamond out of his top pocket and thrust it towards her, but he was holding it tight at the same time. 'Do you know how much this cost? Do you know how much I've done for you?'

'You've been…' How to say he'd been wonderful? He had, but right now it didn't seem like it.

'I've sacrificed everything,' he yelled. 'Everything. Do you think I wanted to practice in a dump like Banksia Bay? Do you know how much money I could have earned if I'd stayed in Sydney? But here I am, doing the books of the Banksia Bay yacht club, stuck here, seeing the same people over and over, even mowing your parents' lawn.'

'I could never figure out why you offered to do that,' she whispered, but he wasn't listening.

'I've done everything, and you throw it all away. For this?' His tone was incredulous. He was staring at Raff as if he were pond scum. 'A Finn.'

'There's some pretty nice Finns,' she said mildly and Raff grinned and tugged her a little closer. Just a little, but Philip noticed.

'You'd leave me for this…this…'

'For Raff,' she said and she gazed steadily at Philip and she even found it in her to feel sorry for him. 'I'm sorry, Philip, but I'm not who you think I am. I've tried…really hard…to be what everyone wants me to be, but I've figured it out. I'm not that person. I'm Abby and I love bright clothes and sleeping in on Sunday and I hate business dinners and I don't like spending my whole life in legal chambers. I like dogs and…'

'Dogs,' Philip snarled. The new, brave Kleppy with his brave new life had emerged from behind Abby's legs and was nosing round Philip's feet, checking him out for smells. Philip looked down at him with loathing. 'That's what this is about. A dog.'

'I know you don't like dogs,' Abby said. 'It was generous of you to say you'd take him…'

'Generous?' He gave a laugh that made her wince. 'Yeah.

I'd even put up with *that*.' The word made her know exactly what he thought of Kleppy.

'Because you love me?' she asked in a small voice and Raff's hand tightened around hers.

'Love.' Philip was staring at her as if she'd lost her mind. 'What's love got to do with it?'

'I…everything.'

'You have no clue. Not one single clue. Enough. You and your parents have messed with my life for ten years. That's it. I've paid a thousandfold. I'm out of here, and if I never see this place again I'll be delighted.'

He turned away, fast, only Kleppy was in the way. He tripped and almost fell. Kleppy yelped.

Philip regained his feet but Kleppy was still between him and his car. And suddenly…

'No,' Raff snapped, but it was too late. They were both too late.

Philip's foot swung back and he kicked. All the frustration and rage of the last two days was in that kick and Kleppy copped it all.

The little dog flew about eight feet, squealing in pain and shock.

'Kleppy!' Abby screamed and ran for him, but Philip moved, too, heading for another kick. Abby launched herself at him, throwing herself down between boot and dog.

Philip grabbed her by the hair and hauled her back… And then suddenly he wasn't there any more. Raff's body was between hers and Philip's. Raff's fist came into contact with Philip—she didn't know where; she couldn't see—but she heard a sickening thud, she saw Philip lurch backwards, stumble, and she saw Raff follow him down.

He had him on the ground, on his stomach, his arm twisted up behind his back, and Philip was screaming…

'Lie still or I'll really hurt you,' Raff said in a voice she didn't recognise. 'Abby, the dog…'

She turned back to Kleppy but Kleppy was no longer there.

He'd backed away in terror. Whining. Horrified, she saw him bolt under the fence and into the undergrowth beyond.

He was yelping in pain and fear and he ran until he was out of sight.

She couldn't catch him. Beyond Raff's fence was Black Mountain. Wilderness.

'Kleppy,' she yelled uselessly into the bushland, but he was gone.

She turned and stared back at Philip with loathing and distress. 'You kicked him.'

'He's a stray.'

'He's mine. I can't believe…' She gulped and turned back to the fence, knowing to try and follow the little dog into the bush would be futile.

'He was running,' Raff said. He was hauling Philip to his feet, none too gentle. 'If he's running, he can't be too badly injured.'

'More's the pity,' Philip snarled, and Raff wrenched him over to the Porsche with a ruthlessness Abby had never seen before. He shoved him into his driver's seat like she'd seen cops put villains into squad cars, only this was Philip's car and he was sending him away.

Or not. Before Philip could guess what he intended, Raff grabbed the keys to Philip's car and tossed them as far as he could, out into the bush.

'You've lost your keys,' he said conversationally. 'Abby, get the handcuffs. They're in the compartment on the passenger side of the patrol car.'

'What…?' she said, and Raff sighed.

'You want to hold your fiancé or get the cuffs.'

'He's not my fiancé.' It seemed important.

'Sorry,' he said. 'Get the cuffs, Abby.' Then, as she glanced despairingly at the fence, he softened. 'Cuffs first. Kleppy second. Move.'

She moved and thirty seconds later Philip was cuffed to his own steering wheel.

'You can't do this,' he snarled.

'Watch me,' Raff said. Then he lifted his radio. 'Keith? You know we were getting a search warrant for Dexter, thinking it might be better to do it when he wasn't home? I have another suggestion. You come up to my place and pick him up. He's cuffed to the car in the driveway. He kicked a dog, pulled Abby's hair. Take him to the station, charge him with aggravated cruelty to animals, plus assault. I'll be there with details when I can but meanwhile he stays in the cells. The paperwork could take quite some time.'

'You…'

'Talk among yourself, Dexter,' he said. 'Abby and I have things to do. Dogs to rescue. And if I find he's badly hurt…' His look said it all. 'Come on, Abby, let's go. He'll be headed for Isaac's and I hope for all our sakes we find him.'

They drove in silence. There was so much to say. On top of her fear for Kleppy, there was so much to think about. Philip's invective…

Philip's words.

I've paid a thousandfold. It was a statement that made her foundations shift from under her.

She cast a look at Raff and his face was set and grim. Had he heard? Was he thinking about it?

Philip… But her thoughts kaleidoscoped back to Kleppy.

'He can't be too badly hurt.'

'No,' Raff said. 'He can't be. He's a dog who's given me my life back. I owe him more than putting Dexter behind bars.'

Where? Where?

They reached Isaac's place and it was fenced and padlocked as it had been fenced and padlocked since Isaac's death.

All the way up the mountain she'd held her breath, hoping Kleppy would be standing at the gate, his nose pressed against the wire. He wasn't.

She called. They both called.

No Kleppy.

'We've come fast on the track,' Raff said. 'Kleppy's having to manage undergrowth.'

'He could be lost.'

'Not Kleppy. Our farm is on his route down to town from here, his route to his source of stolen goods. He'll know every inch.'

'If he's hurt he could creep into the undergrowth and…'

Raff tugged her tight and held her close. 'He was running,' he said. 'If he's not here in ten minutes I'll start bush bashing.' He tugged her tighter still and kissed her, hard and fast. Enormously comforting. Enormously…right. 'If we don't have him in an hour I'll organise a posse,' he said. 'We'll have an army of volunteers up here before nightfall.'

'For Kleppy?'

'We have two things going for us,' Raff said, and his smile was designed to reassure. 'First, Kleppy's one of Henrietta's dogs. She hates having them put down. She's over the moon that you're taking him, and she has a team of volunteers she'll have searching in a heartbeat. Second, if I happen to mention to about half this town that if we find an injured dog we'll put Dexter behind bars… How many raised hands do you reckon we'd get?'

'Is he that bad?' she said in a small voice.

'You know he is.'

She did know it. The thought made her feel…appalled.

What had she been thinking, to drift towards marriage? She'd been in a bad dream that had lasted for years. Of all the stupid…

'Don't kick yourself,' Raff said. 'We all have dumb youthful romances.'

She tried to laugh. She couldn't. A youthful romance that lasted for ten years?

'I seem to remember I did have a youthful romance.'

'Yeah,' he said. They were walking the perimeter now, checking. 'I should have come home and been your partner at the deb ball.'

She did choke on that one. Her debutante ball. The source of all the trouble.

She'd been seventeen years old. A girl had to have a really cool partner for that.

Raff had been in Sydney. She'd been annoyed that he couldn't drive home twice a week to practice, two hours here, two hours back, just to be her partner. Of all the selfish...

'Don't kick yourself,' he said again. 'Dexter does the kicking. Not us.'

'But why?' It was practically a wail. Why?

She'd always assumed Philip loved her. He'd given up Sydney, he'd come home, he'd been the devoted boyfriend, the devoted fiancé for ten years.

Why, if he didn't love her?

'Let's walk down to the road,' Raff said, taking her hand. He held her close, not letting her go for a moment as they walked down the driveway to the gravel road where their world had turned upside down ten years ago.

'Kleppy?' she yelled and then paused. 'Did you hear?'

'Call again.'

She did and there was no mistaking it. A tiny yelp, and then the sound of scuffling.

She was off the road and into the bush, with Raff close behind. Through the undergrowth. Pushing through...

And there he was. Kleppy.

Digging.

Philip's kick had hit his side. She could see grazed skin and blood on his wiry coat.

He looked up from where he'd been digging and wagged his tail and she came close to bursting into tears.

'Klep...'

But he was back digging, dirt going in all directions. His whole body was practically disappearing into the hole he was creating.

'You don't need a wombat,' she told him, feeling almost ill with relief. She reached him and knelt, not caring about the spray of dirt that showered her. 'Klep...'

He tugged back from inside his hole. He had something. He was trying to hold it in his mouth and front paws, tugging it up as he tried to find purchase with his back legs.

She didn't care if it was a dead wombat, buried for years. She gathered him into her arms, mindful of his injured side, and lifted him from the hole.

He snuffled against her, a grubby, bleeding rapscallion of a dog, quivering with delight that she'd found him and, better still, he had something to give her. He wiggled around in her arms and dropped his treasure onto the ground in front of her.

Raff was with her then, ruffling Kleppy's head, smiling his gorgeous, loving smile that made her heart twist inside. How could she have ever walked away from this man for Philip? Like Kleppy's buried treasure, his smile had been waiting for her to rediscover it.

She had rediscovered it.

She wasn't going to marry Philip. Raff was smiling at her. The thought made her feel giddy with happiness.

'Hey,' Raff said in a voice that was none too steady and he gathered them both into his arms. He held them, just held them. His woman, with dog in between.

Happiness was right now.

But there was only so much happiness a small dog could submit to. He submitted for a whole minute before wriggling his nose free and then the rest of him. He started barking, indignation personified, because Abby hadn't taken any interest in his treasure.

Too bad. Raff was kissing her. She had treasure of her own to be finding.

But Kleppy was nothing if not insistent. He was hauling his loot up onto her knees. It was a dirt-covered box, a little damaged at one corner, but not much. It was pencil-box sized, or maybe a little bigger.

She took it and brushed the worst of the dirt off—and then she stilled.

This box.

Philip's box.

No. Philip's grandfather's box. He made boxes like this for all his relations, for all his friends.

This one, though... The shape...

Slowly now, with a lot more care, she dusted the thing off. It was almost totally intact. Cedar did that. It lasted for generations. Something had nibbled at the corner but had given up in disgust.

Cedar was pretty much bug-proof. Obviously it tasted bad. Except to Kleppy.

It would have been the smell, she thought, the distinctive scent, showing him that something was buried here, something like the box he loved back at her place.

'What is it?' Raff was watching her face, figuring this was important.

'I'm not sure,' she said, hardly daring to breathe. A box. Made by Philip's grandfather. Buried not fifty yards from where Ben had been killed.

A box she might just know.

Her fingers were suddenly trembling. Raff took the box from her. 'A bomb?' There was the beginning of a smile in his voice.

'No,' she whispered and then thought about it. 'Maybe.'

'You want me to open it?'

'I think we must.'

There were four brass clips holding it sealed. Raff flicked open each clip in turn.

He opened the box, but she knew before she saw it what its contents would be. And she was right. She'd seen it before. It held cassette tapes, filed neatly, slotted against each other in the ridged sections of Huon pine that Philip's grandpa had carved with such skill.

She didn't need to take them out to know what they were. Music tapes, with a couple of blank ones at the back.

There was an odd one. Not slotted into place. The ribbon had been ripped from its base and the tape looked as if it had been tossed into the box in a hurry. It wasn't labelled.

Her mind was in overdrive.

What do you do when you're panicking?

You grab the tape from the player, rip the ribbon out, throw it into the box with the others that might point to the fact that this tape might exist, and then you head into the bush. You bury it fast, deep in the undergrowth.

And then you come back to the car and you face the fact that a friend is dead and two others injured...

Even if you tried to find it later, you might not. It'd take Kleppy's sense of smell...

But why?

'I'm guessing what this might be,' she said bleakly, and she knew she had to take this further. She was feeling sick. 'Do you think we could still play it?'

'It looks like it's just a matter of reattaching the ribbon. Is it important?'

'I think it might be.'

CHAPTER THIRTEEN

THEY took Kleppy to the vet and Fred declared he'd live. While he did, Raff made a quick call to Keith.

'Dexter's nicely locked up and he's staying that way,' Keith said. 'I have a team organised to swarm through his files. You look after Abby.'

'How did he know you and I…?' Abby said and Raff grinned and shook his head.

'Banksia Bay. Don't ask.'

With his wound cleaned and dressed, they took Kleppy back to Raff's. An hour later, a hearty meal demolished, Kleppy was watching television with Sarah. Lionel was with them. He'd just sort of turned up.

'Heard Kleppy got kicked,' he muttered, and Abby thought, *How does this town do it?*

Abby and Raff were in the back room, standing over Gran's ancient tape player. Waiting for a repaired cassette to start.

Abby felt sick.

Raff was curious. Worried. Watching her. She hadn't told him what to expect. It might not be anything.

But why was it buried there if it wasn't anything?

And as soon as it started she knew she was right, at least in thinking she knew what it was.

She'd watched Philip over the years as he'd recorded his client discussions—'in case I miss something'. She'd attributed it to his meticulous preparation.

She'd believed him, all those years ago when she'd found

the Christabelle tape. She'd used it as a reason to break up with him, but had hardly thought any more of it. But in the box buried by the roadside where Ben died…there was more evidence.

Maybe Philip taped all his girlfriends.

For this was Sarah, ten years younger but still unmistakably herself. Young and excited and a little bit nervous.

It had been set to record as soon as Philip picked her up, and they knew immediately it was the night of the crash. They listened to Sarah asking if they could go up the mountain and see if the boys had their car going.

'Sure.' Philip was amenable. 'I wouldn't count on it going, though. Let's show 'em what a real car can do. You like my wheels?'

'Your car's great.' But even from the distance of ten years they could hear Sarah's increasing nervousness, from almost as soon as they started driving. 'Philip, slow down. These curves are dangerous.'

'I can handle them. It's Raff and Ben who should worry. They can hardly drive.'

More talk. Sarah asked if he liked her dress. Even then, Philip wasn't into bright dresses.

'Not so much. Why'd it have to be red?'

A terse response. Sarah sounded peeved.

'Movies afterwards?' Philip asked.

'I'm not sure. If you don't like my dress sense…'

'There's no need to be touchy.'

Silence. An offended huff? Then Sarah again…

'Phil, be careful. That was a wallaby.'

'It's fine. Wallabies are practically plague round here, anyway. Why are they using the fire track?'

'They can't go on the roads. Their car isn't registered.'

'That hunk of junk'll never get registered. Not like this baby. Watch it go.'

'Philip, no. Slow down. You're scaring me. There'll be more wallabies—it's getting dark.'

'There's nothing to be scared of. You reckon they're on this track?'

'Philip… Philip, no. You nearly hit it…' And then… 'You're on the wrong side of the…'

'There's ruts on the other side. No one uses this.'

'But it's a crest.' Her voice rose. 'Philip, it's a crest. No…'

Then…awfulness.

Then nothing. Nothing, nothing and nothing.

The tape spun on into silence.

Dear God…

Raff changed colour. Held onto the back of the nearest chair.

She moved then, closing the distance between them in a heartbeat, linking her arms around his chest and tugging him to her. She held him and held him and held him. She'd had some inkling, the moment she'd seen the buried box. But Raff… This was a lightning bolt.

Raff…

He'd been her hero since she was eight years old. He was her wonderful Raff.

Her love.

'I didn't…' he said, and it was as if he was waking from a nightmare. 'I believed Philip. He said I was on the wrong side.'

'That's why there was never a court case,' she whispered. 'The storm hit just as the crash happened. There was only Philip's word.'

They'd believed him. They'd all believed him. It had been so hard—so unthinkable—to do anything else.

She saw it all.

Philip's stupidity had killed Ben; had desperately injured Sarah. He couldn't admit it, but what followed…

Some part of Philip was still decent. He was a kid raised in Banksia Bay, and he'd been their friend in childhood. His parents were friends with her parents. They'd loved Ben to bits.

He'd have been truly appalled.

So a part of him had obviously decided to do the 'right

thing', and in his eyes he had. He'd come back here to practice law, playing the son to her parents, devoting himself to Banksia Bay as Ben would have.

'He's been making amends for Ben,' she said, and she was trying hard to hold back the anger. Raff didn't need her anger now. He just needed…her? 'He came back and tried to make amends to us all.'

And then, despite what she'd intended, anger hit, a wave so great it threatened to overwhelm her. 'No. Not to us all. He tried to make amends to me and to my parents. He would have married me, as if that somehow made up for Ben's life. But to you… For ten years he's let you think you were responsible. For ten years he's let you hold the blame.'

Tears were coursing down her cheeks now. She'd thought she was comforting Raff but her rage was so great there was no comfort she could give. If Philip walked in the door right now…

'I'll tear his heart out,' she stammered. 'If he has a heart. I can't bear it. He's lost you years.'

'No.'

Raff put her back from him then, holding her hard by each shoulder. He'd regained his colour and, unbelievably, he was smiling. 'I believe you told me you loved me before you found this tape.'

'Yes, but…'

'Then it's Philip who's lost the ten years. I've faced it and come out the other side.' He took a deep breath. 'Whew. This takes some getting used to.'

'We can tell the world. Oh, Raff… I can't bear anyone thinking a moment longer that you…'

'That I was dumb as a teenager? I *was* dumb,' he said gently. 'I shouldn't have been up there that night. None of us should. I believe I might even cut Philip slack on this one.'

'No!'

'He's lost you,' Raff said and he tugged her against him and let his chin rest on her hair. 'Winner takes all. That'd be me. And I need to think things through before I do anything rash—like spreading this far and wide.'

She stared at him as if he were out of his mind. 'Why on earth…?'

'You know, my reputation does no end of good for my street cred,' he said, thoughtful now. 'How many local kids know the local cop was dumb and someone died because of it? You get experts lecturing kids on speed and they shrug it off. They see how Mrs Fryer treats me? For a cop, that's gold. I reckon it's even saved lives.'

'Raff…'

'Don't think it's not important,' he said, laughter fading. He was holding her at arm's length and meeting her gaze with gravity and truth. 'To look at Sarah now and know I wasn't responsible for her pain… To look at you and know it wasn't me who hurt you… I can't tell you what that means. But Philip has some pretty heavy stuff coming to him anyway. I can cope without my own pound of flesh. Believe me, I can cope.

'All I need I have right here. This tape is a great gift, Abby, but the greatest gift of all is you.'

He tugged her to him then, and he held her, close enough so their heartbeats merged. She was dissolving into him, she thought. She loved this man with all her heart. No matter what he decided to do about this tape, they could go forward from this moment.

'Marry me,' he said and the world stood still.

'Marry?' She could barely get the word out.

'I hear on the grapevine you have a perfectly good wedding dress. I'm a man who hates waste.'

'Raff…'

'Don't quibble,' he said sternly. 'Just say yes.'

'You're in shock. You're emotional. You need time to think.'

He put her away from him again. Held her at arm's length. Smiled.

'I've thought,' he said. 'Marry me.'

'Okay.'

* * *

Okay? As an acceptance of a marriage proposal it lacked a certain finesse but it was a great start. For a lawyer. He found himself laughing, a great explosion of happiness that came from so far within he'd never known that place existed. He lifted her up in his arms and whirled her round as if she weighed nothing.

She did weigh nothing. She was part of him—his Abby, his love.

His…wife?

He set her down, laughter fading. Joy was taking its place, a joy so great he felt he was shedding an old skin and bursting into something new.

She tilted her chin and he kissed her, so slowly, so thoroughly satisfactorily, that words weren't possible. Words weren't needed for a very long time.

She held him tight, she kissed him and she placed her future in his hands. She loved him so much she felt her heart could burst.

He was Banksia Bay's bad boy no longer. He was just… Raff.

If he insisted, then maybe she wouldn't tell the town about Philip, she conceded—but she would tell her parents. And she would tell Philip that she knew. And then… This was Banksia Bay. If things got around… Things always got around.

But right now it was becoming incredibly hard to care. All she cared about was that Raff was holding her as if he'd never let her go. He was kissing her as he'd kissed her when she was sixteen, only more so. A lot more so. He was grown into her man. He was her love, for ever and ever.

'I can't believe this is happening,' he said at last in a voice that was changed, different. It was the voice of a man who was walking into a future he'd never dreamed of. 'Abby, are you sure?' And then he hesitated. 'I do need to care for Sarah.' There was sudden doubt.

'I believe there's room enough here for all of us,' she said, deeply contented. She pulled back enough to peep through to the next room, where Lionel and Sarah were watching television. They were covered in three dogs, two cats and a vast bowl of popcorn. They were looking…self-conscious. On closer inspection… They were holding hands.

'There must be something in the water,' she said and grinned, and Raff tugged her close again, smiling wide enough to make her dissolve in the happiness of his smile.

'So you'd take us all on? This place. And Sarah's dogs and guinea pigs and hens and ponies and…'

'And whoever else comes along,' she said, and chuckled at the look on his face.

He caught his breath. 'You'd…'

'I think I would,' she said, a bubble of joy rising so fast it was threatening to overwhelm her. 'It might be fun.'

'You're talking babies,' he said, feeling his way.

'I believe I am. You know,' she said thoughtfully, 'if we sold my place we could even do up your other house as well as this one.'

He took a deep breath. Looked through to the sitting room. Saw what she was seeing. Sarah and Lionel…

'We might just have found ourselves a gardener,' Abby said, smiling and smiling.

Enough. This was going so fast he was being left behind. A man had to take a stand some time, so he took his stand right there. Right then. A simple *okay* was not satisfactory for what he had in mind. He dropped to one knee. 'Abigail Callahan, will you marry me?'

'I've already said…' she started.

'You said *okay*. I don't think *okay*'s legally binding.'

'You want me to prepare contracts?'

'In triplicate.'

She smiled down at him, for how could she help it? She smiled and smiled. And then she thought this moment called for gravitas. It was a Very Serious Moment. It was the beginning of the rest of her life.

She stepped back and stood a little way away, looking down at him. At all of him.

At this man who'd be her husband.

She could still see him, she thought. The spiky-haired ten-year-old who her eight-year-old self had fallen in love with. That dangerous twinkle...

Her bad boy.

Her love.

'If I turn out to be a sewing mistress instead of a lawyer...' she ventured.

'Suits me.'

'If I'm not struck off the professional roll for this morning's unprofessional conduct I might help out the Crown Prosecutor from time to time.'

'You can't get struck off for dropping a briefcase—and Malcolm surely needs some help. You know, I'm feeling a bit dumb, kneeling over here when you're over there.'

She hadn't finished. 'I do want babies.'

'How many?' he asked and there was a trace of unease in his voice.

'Six,' she said, and laughed at the look on his face.

'Can we try one out for size first?'

'Sounds a plan. Raff...'

'Yes, my love?'

'That's just it,' she said, feeling suddenly...shy. 'My love. Let me say... I need to explain. Only once and then it's over, but I do need to get it out. Raff, I've loved you all the time without stopping but my pain stopped me thinking with my heart. I forced myself to think with my head. That's done. I'm so, so sorry that I can't take back those ten years.'

'Hush,' he said.

'I have to say it.'

'You've said it,' he murmured. 'I don't like to mention it but there's no carpet here. I'm kneeling on wood. I didn't have the forethought to use a cushion. Any more quibbles?'

'No, but...'

He sighed. 'Then how about saying you'll marry me and taking me out of my pain?'

'Okay.'

'Abigail!'

She laughed, and she hardly felt herself cross the distance between them. She knelt to join him and he tugged her close.

He kissed her again, so thoroughly, so wonderfully that doubts, unhappiness, emptiness were gone and she knew they were gone for ever.

'We can't take back those ten years,' he whispered into her hair as the kiss paused before restarting. 'How about we give ourselves the next ten instead?'

'Ten…'

'And the ten after that. And after that, too. Decades and decades of love and family and…'

And something was bumping against her leg.

Kleppy. He was tugging the popcorn bowl to his mistress with care.

She giggled and lifted him up and popcorn went flying. He'd tugged it with such care and she'd spilled it.

Who cared? A lawyer might. Not Abigail Callahan. Not the wife of Banksia Bay's Bad Boy.

'Decades and decades of love and family and dogs,' she said, and Raff took Kleppy firmly from her and set him down so he could kiss her again.

'Definitely, my love. Definitely family, definitely dogs, definitely love. For now and for ever. For as long as we both shall live. So now, Abigail Callahan, for the third and final time, will you marry me? I want more than *okay*. I want properly, soberly, legally, and with all your heart.'

'Why, yes, Rafferty Finn,' she managed between love and laughter. 'Where would you like me to sign?'

Abby didn't wear two thousand beads to her wedding.

For a start, it didn't seem right that she wear a dress she'd prepared for her marriage to Philip. Almost as soon as Raff put a ring on her finger she was planning an alternative.

Rainbows.

So Sarah wore her dress—Sarah, who'd looked at her dress of

two thousand beads and burst into tears. 'It's the most beautiful thing I've ever seen.' And Sarah needed a wedding gown.

For: 'Lionel's not staying in that horrid boarding house a minute longer,' she declared, but Lionel was old-fashioned. He was delighted to move to Raff's farm; he was incredibly happy to start renovating the little house at the rear, but he'd marry his Sarah first.

They were even thinking…if Lionel got his money back from Philip…Isaac's place wasn't so far from the farm. Maybe they could be even more independent.

So Raff gave his sister away. Abby was maid of honour and if she was as weepy as any mother of the bride then who could blame her? Her gown of two thousand beads had found a use she could hardly have dreamed of.

And then it was Abby's turn for her wedding, a month later, but on a day just as wonderful. They were to be married in the church—the church she'd been baptised in, the church Ben had been buried from.

Half Banksia Bay came to see. Even Mrs Fryer.

For things had shifted for the town's bad boy.

Rumours were flying. True to his word, Raff refused to make public the contents of the tape, but the people of Banksia Bay never let lack of evidence get in the way of a good rumour. And there were plenty of pointers saying Raff might well have been misjudged.

For a start, Abby's parents were trying their best to get to know Raff, and suddenly they wouldn't hear a bad word against him. They even offered to move into Raff's house while Raff and Abby went on their honeymoon, in case Lionel needed help with Sarah.

And people remembered. Raff had been judged on Philip's word and nothing else. But now… Philip had abandoned the town and moved to Sydney. He was facing malpractice charges and more.

Philip's parents were appalled. They owned an apartment in Bondi and rumour said they were thinking of moving themselves, leaving Banksia Bay to be with their son.

They were the only ones behind Philip, though. Even Philip's grandpa was right here at the wedding. What was more, at Abby's tentative request he'd made a beautiful box for the ring bearer.

The ring bearer...

Raff stood before the altar waiting for his bride and he couldn't help thinking the choice of ring bearer might be a mistake.

Abby swore it'd be okay. She'd spent hours training him. The plan was for her mother to hold Kleppy, and then, when Raff called, he'd trot across, bearing the ring. What could possibly go wrong?

Who knew, but Raff organised for Keith to carry a backup ring in his pocket. It wasn't that he didn't trust Kleppy.

Um...yes, it was. He stood in the church waiting for his bride and he thought he definitely didn't trust Kleppy.

But suddenly he could no longer focus on Abby's dog. The doors of the church swung open and Abby was right there. Holding her father's hand. Looking along the aisle to find him.

His bride. His Abby.

She'd wanted rainbows, and that was what she was to be married in. She'd made this herself as well, and it was as individual as she was. The gown was soft white silk, almost transparent, floating over panels of pastel hues, every shade a man could imagine. Her tight-fitting bodice clung to her lovely figure and the skirt flared out in clouds of shimmering colour, with the soft-coloured silk shimmering from underneath.

She was so beautiful...

She wore her hair simply, no longer in the elegant chignon he'd hated for years, but dropping in tendrils to her bare shoulders. She wore a simple halo of fresh flowers in her hair—and she took his breath away.

Sarah followed her in, proud fit to burst. Matron of honour. She wore a matching dress, also rainbow-coloured but without the translucent overskirt that made Abby seem to float.

Sarah was also supposed to be wearing a ring of flowers in

her hair, but that had been the one hiccup of the morning. 'It might give me a headache,' she'd said, doubtful.

'Why don't you take it and leave it in the car?' Raff had suggested. 'That way, you can wear it for the official photographs and take it off if it starts hurting.'

She'd approved his suggestion. She was happy now, bareheaded, beautiful, a married woman, fussing over her best friend's gown.

She wasn't as happy as Raff. Not possible. His Abby was smiling at him. His Abby was about to be his wife.

What could be more perfect?

The music filled the church. Abby's father led her forward, beaming with pride, and Raff stepped forward to receive his bride.

His Abby.

What could go wrong with today?

Kleppy could go wrong.

There was a scuffle in the front pew. Abby's mother had retired behind her handkerchief and forgotten her Kleppy-clutching duty. She made a wild grab but it was too late: he was free.

Kleppy was groomed to an inch of his life. He was wearing a bow of the same rainbow-coloured fabric lining Abby's gown.

He was off and running.

He trotted straight up the aisle, tail high, a dog on a mission—and he disappeared out of the door.

Uh-oh. What was a cop supposed to do now? What was a groom supposed to do?

'Leave him to me,' Keith growled, setting a hand firmly on Raff's shoulder. 'Lights and sirens. Handcuffs. Padded cell if necessary. I'll pull him in no time.'

'Kleppy,' Abby faltered.

'You two get on with your wedding,' Keith told them, and they looked at each other and knew they must. A hundred people were watching them. These people loved them and they were waiting to see them married.

'But he has the ring,' Abby faltered.

'We have backup,' Keith said and handed Raff the spare.

'Oh, Raff…' He could tell she didn't know whether to be thankful or indignant.

'It's not that I didn't trust him,' Raff said—unconvincingly—and then he paused.

Kleppy was back. With a ring.

He had two rings now, the plain band of gold in the tiny box hanging round his neck—and Sarah's halo of flowers, left on the front seat of the bridal carriage.

It was a ring of fresh flowers to match Abby's.

He carried it straight to Abby and sat and wagged his tail and waited to be told how good he was.

'He's brought us a ring,' Abby said and choked.

The congregation was choking as well—or laughing out loud. Kleppy's reputation had grown considerably in the last couple of months.

But Raff had his priorities in order now. There were things to be done before he acknowledged his soon-to-be wife's dog. He took her hands in his, tugged her to face him and lightly kissed her. 'You,' he told her, 'are the most beautiful woman in the world.'

'You make my toes curl,' she said.

There was a light 'harrumph' from before them. They were, after all, here to get married.

Raff smiled and stooped and held out his hand, and Kleppy laid his ring of flowers into his palm. He lifted it up and gave it to Abby.

'I guess this is Kleppy's wedding gift.'

'I'll treasure it for always,' she managed.

'You should. For with this ring, I thee wed,' he said softly. 'With this dog, I thee marry. Before this community, with these friends, I pledge you my troth.'

There was a murmur of delighted approval.

Abby was looking…in love.

Kleppy, however, was still looking expectant.

Raff knelt and lifted the small gold band from the box

around Kleppy's neck. He pocketed it carefully—and then he placed the ring of flowers around Kleppy's neck.

'Sarah,' he said to his sister. 'Can you hold Kleppy? I have things to do.'

'Sure,' Sarah said, beaming. 'Lionel will help me.'

So Sarah and Lionel held Kleppy. Raff took Abby's hands in his and he faced her—a man facing his woman on their wedding day.

'Enough,' he said softly, for her ears alone. 'Dogs have their place, as do sisters and friends and flowers. But for now... Are you ready to marry me?'

'If you'll take me. And my crazy dog.'

'We'll take whatever comes with both of us,' he told her, strongly and firmly. 'As long as we have each other.'

'Oh, yes.' She smiled at him mistily through tears. He kissed her again, lightly on the lips—and then the ceremony began as it was meant to begin. As Rafferty Finn and Abigail Callahan stood together, in peace and in love, to become one.

Harlequin® Romance

Coming Next Month

Available June 14, 2011

#4243 BABY ON THE RANCH
Susan Meier
Babies in the Boardroom

#4244 AND BABY MAKES THREE
Rebecca Winters and Lucy Gordon

#4245 ORDINARY GIRL IN A TIARA
Jessica Hart
The Princess Swap

#4246 TEMPTED BY TROUBLE
Liz Fielding

#4247 MISTY AND THE SINGLE DAD
Marion Lennox
Banksia Bay

#4248 HER MOMENT IN THE SPOTLIGHT
Nina Harrington

You can find more information on upcoming
Harlequin® titles, free excerpts and more at
www.HarlequinInsideRomance.com.

REQUEST YOUR FREE BOOKS!
2 FREE NOVELS PLUS 2 FREE GIFTS!

From the Heart, For the Heart

HRI1

Harlequin® Blaze™ brings you
New York Times *and* USA TODAY *bestselling author*
Vicki Lewis Thompson with three new steamy titles
from the bestselling miniseries SONS OF CHANCE

Chance isn't just the last name of these rugged
Wyoming cowboys—it's their motto, too!

Read on for a sneak peek at the first title,
SHOULD'VE BEEN A COWBOY

Available June 2011 only from Harlequin® Blaze™.

"THANKS FOR NOT TURNING ON THE LIGHTS," Tyler said. "I'm a mess."

"Not in my book." Even in low light, Alex had a good view of her yellow shirt plastered to her body. It was all he could do not to reach for her, mud and all. But the next move needed to be hers, not his.

She slicked her wet hair back and squeezed some water out of the ends as she glanced upward. "I like the sound of the rain on a tin roof."

"Me, too."

She met his gaze briefly and looked away. "Where's the sink?"

"At the far end, beyond the last stall."

Tyler's running shoes squished as she walked down the aisle between the rows of stalls. She glanced sideways at Alex. "So how much of a cowboy are you these days? Do you ride the range and stuff?"

"I ride." He liked being able to say that. "Why?"

"Just wondered. Last summer, you were still a city boy. You even told me you weren't the cowboy type, but you're…different now."

He wasn't sure if that was a good thing or a bad thing. Maybe she preferred city boys to cowboys. "How am I different?"

"Well, you dress differently, and your hair's a little longer. Your face seems a little more chiseled, but maybe that's because of your hair. Also, there's something else, something harder to define, an attitude…"

"Are you saying I have an attitude?"

"Not in a bad way. It's more like a quiet confidence."

He was flattered, but still he had to laugh. "I just admitted a while ago that I have all kinds of doubts about this event tomorrow. That doesn't seem like quiet confidence to me."

"This isn't about your job, it's about…your…" She took a deep breath. "It's about your sex appeal, okay? I have no business talking about it, because it will only make me want to do things I shouldn't do." She started toward the end of the barn. "Now, where's that sink? We need to get cleaned up and go back to the house. Dinner is probably ready, and I—"

He spun her around and pulled her into his arms, mud and all. "Let's do those things." Then he kissed her, knowing that she would kiss him back, knowing that this time he would take that kiss where he wanted it to go. And she would let him.

Follow Tyler and Alex's wild adventures in
SHOULD'VE BEEN A COWBOY
Available June 2011 only from Harlequin® Blaze™
wherever books are sold.

SPECIAL EDITION

Life, Love and Family

LOVE CAN BE FOUND IN THE MOST UNLIKELY PLACES, ESPECIALLY WHEN YOU'RE NOT LOOKING FOR IT...

Failed marriages, broken families and disappointment. Cecilia and Brandon have both been unlucky in love and life and are ripe for an intervention. Good thing Brandon's mother happens to stumble upon this matchmaking project. But will Brandon be able to open his eyes and get away from his busy career to see that all he needs is right there in front of him?

FIND OUT IN
WHAT THE SINGLE DAD WANTS...

BY *USA TODAY* BESTSELLING AUTHOR
MARIE FERRARELLA

AVAILABLE IN JUNE 2011
WHEREVER BOOKS ARE SOLD.

www.eHarlequin.com

SE0611MF